CAPTURED BY THE ALIEN WARRIOR

HOPE HART

The Arcav Alien Invasion Series

The Arcav King's Mate

The Arcav Commander's Human

The Arcav General's Woman

The Arcav Prince's Captive

A Very Arcav Christmas

The Arcav Captain's Queen

The Arcav Guard's Female

The Warriors of Agron Series

Taken by the Alien Warrior

Claimed by the Alien Warrior

Saved by the Alien Warrior

Seduced by the Alien Warrior

Protected by the Alien Warrior

Captured by the Alien Warrior

Rescued by the Alien Warrior

Enticed by the Alien Warrior

CHAPTER ONE

D ragix

I have been alone for centuries. Sometimes, I imagine what it would be like to be surrounded by others of my kind on this planet. But today, the very thought is laughable. Life is monotony.

At least it was until just a few moments ago, when a huge metal object slammed into the ground.

I know metal. It was this material that the Braxians used to kill my parents.

I watch for a while, but nothing happens. Finally, the yellow two-legs approach. I snort, a small plume of smoke escaping my left nostril. The yellow ones taste bitter, their bones splintering easily.

I leave, no longer interested. I fly over my territory, scanning the forest for anything that will hold my attention. Truthfully, this entire planet is mine, yet I do not often care to leave my favorite mountain, with the large, flat rock so perfect for napping in the afternoon sun.

I bank left, flexing my wings as I turn my attention to my next meal.

I do not concern myself with two-legs.

Charlie

I think I may be dying.

I've been hit in the head plenty of times before—the consequences of living with a man who thought it was A-okay to smack me in the face when I displeased him.

This is something different. My head feels wrong. And there's so much blood. I can smell it all over me, the scent metallic even through the bitter smell of the vomit I just left on the ground in front of me.

We've been walking for hours. Following the yellow creatures who say they're taking us back to their tribe to help us find food and water.

At this point, it takes every ounce of my energy just to put one foot in front of the other. The other women are flicking me concerned glances, but I have no choice except to follow the herd like a wounded sheep, waiting to be picked off by a wolf.

I snort at that, and my head spins as I stumble over a tree root sticking up from the ground. I just need a few minutes. Just a moment or two to catch my breath and hope that the world stops spinning sickly around me.

"I need a break," I manage to get out. One of the other women—Ellie, I think her name is—glances at me, and her mouth drops open. Her face pales as she glances at my head and then back at Karok—the leader of the Voildi.

He doesn't look impressed. "We must keep moving if we are to make it to our camp by nightfall."

Nevada—a tough, confident woman who told us she's a marine—gives him a long look.

"Charlie isn't feeling well," she says. "We can take ten minutes."

The other women stop, and I reach out, leaning against one of the trees. The white bark is rough under my hand, and I take deep breaths, fighting against the nausea as I hear Ellie begging the Voildi to help us find some water.

Water.

I'd give just about anything for just a cupped handful of water right now.

I don't know what the Voildi say in reply, but from the tension I can feel rolling off the other women, it's not good.

And then I'm stumbling back, fighting against the roiling in my stomach as several huge, long-haired, *seriously* muscled men jump into the small clearing and draw their swords, eyes narrowed on the Voildi.

"Great," I mutter, too sick to even be afraid. "Just fucking *great*."

I don't want to die. I haven't even truly *lived* yet. So I turn, scanning the clearing behind me as I attempt to find a hiding spot. I'm well aware of my limitations, and from the sound of metal clashing, I can already tell that my self-defense class is useless here.

I back away. If I have to choose between dying from a head wound and being struck through with one of those huge swords, I'm going to choose option A. It involves curling up and going to sleep, and right now, that sounds just peachy.

I frantically scan my surroundings, finding a small path between several of the tall, bleached trees. I use them to steady myself as I stumble away, searching for somewhere safe to hunker down and hide.

The further I get from the sound of men fighting—and dying—in that clearing, the more certain I am that I can hear water rushing in the distance.

Maybe this can be my contribution to the group, since I'm not exactly contributing much else. If the other women are smart, they'll be hiding as well. And if we all live through the next few moments, I can at least direct them to water.

It's this thought that makes me increase my stumbling pace. The blood pounds in my ears as I trip over sharp sticks and rocks, without the energy to even wince in pain.

And that's when the creature strikes.

I scream as something hits me from behind, and I'm falling, but right before I hit the ground, I'm lifted up, up into the fern-colored sky.

Claws. Those are claws holding me, pressed into my skin. Within a second, my body flips, my legs rising, until I'm falling backward.

"Oh God, oh God, oh God."

Just like I imagined. The wounded, bleeding sheep was picked off from the herd.

I really wish I'd just found a nice spot to fall asleep and let the head wound do its job.

When my body begins to flip, I squeeze my eyes shut. I'm definitely about to be thrust into the creature's mouth. The last sound I'll hear will be the *crunch* of what are sure to be sharp teeth as it bites down on my body.

I shudder, but the creature isn't eating me yet. Instead, I

feel something beneath me, something warm. The claws let go, and I plop onto...scales.

I glance up, and my stomach roils as my mouth goes dry. I thought I was in trouble before, but this is much worse.

The creature holding me cupped in its hand or foot is a...dragon.

I reach up a shaky hand and prod at my head. Pain explodes through my scalp and into my brain, and I yelp.

Still alive. Not dreaming.

The dragon's scales are blue. No...green. No...both. His wings cast a shadow over me, and I glance down. The ground is spinning, that huge shadow demonstrating the wingspan of the beast.

Too far to jump.

The hand...or foot curls around me, the huge claws rising as if the dragon has read my mind. I look up again, and I can't help but tremble as it tilts its head, one bright gold eye narrowing as it examines me.

I lean over and vomit, getting most of it on the creature's scales. I raise my head in time to see a curl of smoke rise from one of the dragon's nostrils as it chuffs.

My head swims, and I finally lean back, too sick to care that I'm about to be eaten.

***

Dragix

The female creature slumps against me, and I fly faster. I can smell her blood through the underlying sickness that seems to radiate from her.

If I do not get her back to my lair quickly, she will die. I tilt my head at that. When I swooped down to collect the strange two-legged female, I thought I was drawn to her scent for a meal.

No. The female creature smells good but not for eating.

She smells like...family. Like laughter and joy. Like fighting and mating.

My mountain looms in the distance, and I pick up the pace, catching an air current as I soar through the sky.

When I approach the long, flat rock, I ensure that my landing is soft, unwilling to further jostle my new possession.

The female groans weakly against me, and I waste no time. I place her gently on the ground and get to work, licking at her bleeding.

My saliva will heal most wounds, but it cannot bring back the dead. And I can hear the dull *thump* of this female's heart, the beats spaced further and further apart, as if it is close to giving up.

I glance up, narrowing my eyes at the movement as Maez steps through the rocky entrance to my lair. If she is surprised to see the wounded creature on the rock in front of me, she doesn't show it, instead dropping her eyes submissively.

I wait one long moment. Maez has served me faithfully, as her kind once served and lived in harmony with my people. When the Braxians came, my race was not the only race to be slaughtered.

I give her a warning look as she raises her eyes, and she waits for my nod before she approaches. I don't need to tell her that this creature is not for eating. She angles her head, her gaze immediately falling on the wounded female's head.

"Oh no," she murmurs, crouching down next to her. "She is very close to death, Dragix."

I snort, and she glances up at my displeasure.

"You expect honesty, and I'm giving it to you. She may not last the night."

I narrow my eyes again, and Maez sighs.

"So much blood," she tuts. Her hands are gentle as she moves the female's hair away from the deep wound. I reach out one claw to feel her hair. When I let go, the black lock bounces back into place.

"Curls," Maez says, but her attention is elsewhere. She frowns as she examines the female's ear, where blood has pooled. "There's a small break in her skull here...see? If you want her to live..." She raises her eyes as if checking that this is still correct, and I nod. "In that case, you'll need to ensure your saliva gets deep right here. If her bone can knit back together and her brain is not injured, she will survive."

I nod and get to work, licking at the injury. Maez directs me, and I ensure that my saliva is deep enough to heal.

This healing is one of the many reasons creatures on this planet attempt to hunt me. They believe it is my blood that can heal almost any injury.

I return my attention to the female. Maez murmurs something about water and steps away. When she has returned, I am finished, and I watch as she manages to trickle a few sips of water down the female's throat.

"Now all we can do is wait," Maez says, and I resist the urge to snarl at her. She has been the one loyal creature in my life for years now. If she says that there is no more to do, I will believe her.

She leaves me with the strange female, and since Maez has wiped some of the blood away, I can examine her properly. The female's skin is white and pallid, and her body is much smaller than the other two-legs' on this planet. I don't know the color of her eyes, and I find myself interested, wishing she would open them so I can see.

It is worth keeping this two-leg alive for that curiosity alone. I have not felt interest in anything other than the sun on my scales and the occasional hunt for...too long.

If this two-leg breaks the boredom of my long life, then I will keep her.

CHAPTER TWO

C harlie

I wake to warmth. Someone is bathing my face, and the feeling of anyone touching me with gentleness is strange enough that my eyes pop open.

One huge gold eye stares back at me.

I yelp, pushing my hands into the hard rock beneath me as I attempt to sit up.

The dragon.

Oh God. He hasn't eaten me yet. Maybe he prefers his prey conscious.

My hands shake at the thought. Why can I never catch a break? Now instead of dying while unconscious, I get to do it while completely aware of what's about to happen to me?

No one has my kind of luck. No one.

The dragon lowers his head again, and I yelp as I realize that he's been *licking me.* I'm suddenly enraged, and I lift my hand, pushing his head away.

That dinner-plate-sized eye narrows on me.

This bastard thinks he can play with his prey? Can lick my blood and enjoy torturing me slowly as I die?

I don't think so.

He leans down again, and this time, I punch him in the snout.

His eye widens, and he rears back. I use the opportunity to turn onto my hands and knees, attempting to crawl along the hard rock.

Within the blink of an eye, the dragon is in front of me. He's so huge that he only had to swivel his head around to stare down at me.

He wants to savor his kill? I'll piss him off enough that he ends me quick. Sometimes you gotta take your wins where you find them.

He leans down again, and I bare my teeth at him.

He simply opens his mouth slightly to display his own.

Oh God. His teeth. They're packed into that lethal mouth like sharp knives in a drawer.

He leans closer again, likely believing that showing me those sharp white teeth is enough to make me fall in line with his plan to eat me in small bites.

This time, I aim for his eye.

He slams it closed in time, but my fist hits the flesh of his eyelid. It's thick and strong, but it must still be sensitive because the dragon leans back his head and roars.

His eyes are enraged when he looks down at me again.

"He's trying to heal you," a voice says, and the dragon turns his head, the movement allowing me to see a woman. She has long white hair, and her skin is a light purple. I glance back at the predator in front of me, more interested in keeping him in my line of sight.

"He's licking at my blood. What is it, an appetizer for him?"

The woman laughs softly, her voice sounding closer. The dragon tilts his head at her, once again showing off his teeth. Or is it *her* teeth? No. The woman just called the beast "him."

"If he wanted to eat you, you'd already be in his belly," she says. "Believe me when I say that he's trying to help you heal."

"Why would he do that?"

"He does as he pleases."

I can practically feel the shrug in her voice even as I keep my eyes on the dragon, who is looking more pissed off by the second. He doesn't like us talking, I realize.

"This doesn't exactly seem hygienic."

"Dragon saliva has incredible healing properties. I suggest you allow him to tend to your wound."

"I don't think I can."

To lie here like prey and allow this creature to lick at my blood? That's too much to ask.

I return my gaze to the woman, and the smell of smoke fills my nostrils as the dragon shifts.

"Look," I say, attempting to make them see reason. "I'm feeling much better."

I am, I realize. I no longer want to curl into a ball and vomit repeatedly, and my vision isn't blurred. Best of all, the world isn't swimming around me. My head still pounds, the headache relentless, but if I can get away from here, I might actually have a chance of living.

She raises her eyebrow, and I narrow my eyes at her.

"I'm grateful for whatever has happened here, but I need to get back to the other women I was with."

What if they've found a way off this godforsaken planet? What if they leave without me?

It's that thought that makes me attempt to rise once more, and the dragon makes it clear that this displeases him, shoving his huge face so close to mine that my fist itches to punch him again.

"Dragix does as he pleases," the woman says again over my shoulder, and I can hear her footsteps fade as she walks away.

Dragix

The two-leg is not pleased. She glances after Maez, her eyes widening as if she has been betrayed.

"Obviously the sisterhood doesn't exist on this planet," she mutters.

She returns her attention to me. "If you can understand me, blink once."

I am...entertained. I blink, and her eyes widen further.

They're a deep blue. So blue that they remind me of the Colossal Water when the sun hits it in the morning. The color soothes me, dampening the endless rage that beats within my body like a drum.

"Okay," the female says. "My name is Charlie. Well, it's really Charlotte, but my friends call me Charlie. You can call me that too, if you promise not to eat me."

Char-lee. I have never heard such a name. I cannot speak to her, I... mourn this. I blink at her instead, and she gives me a trembling smile. I can still smell her terror, but she is attempting to dampen it. Brave creature.

"Look," she says. "I appreciate the *healing.*" Her lips

twists, and she stares at my mouth as if slightly revolted. "But I don't need that anymore. So if you could keep your healing powers to yourself, that would be much appreciated."

I snort, and she flinches as a curl of smoke escapes my nostril. Her eyes widen, the air thick with her fear.

She is still in pain. Even if I couldn't smell it, lingering below her terror, I can see it in the way her eyes close and she flinches each time I move my head and the sun hits her eyes.

I didn't go through all the trouble of snatching up this female only to have her die before I can understand why I am so intrigued by her. I did not finally find an escape from the endless boredom and rage only for her weak two-leg body to fail.

I lean down, attempting to ignore the scent of her dread. Usually, the smell of fear is heady, an appetizer before I eat my prey. Her fear is different. It makes me want to roar, to burn whoever made her bleed.

I freeze. Two-legs are fragile; however, they do not bleed with no reason. For the first time, my inability to communicate with this female—with *Charlie*—frustrates me. Someone must have caused her injuries. I will find out who, and I will turn them to ash.

I scan her body, noting the black-and-blue bruising along her arms and legs. She has a long cut along her thigh that has reopened with her movement and is slowly oozing blood.

She squeaks as I lean down, and her hand lashes out, attempting to push my head away as I stroke my tongue along the deep cut. Her panic fills the air, and I give her a warning look as she raises her fist once more. I was surprised more than anything when she hit me the first time. But the second time, when she struck my sensitive eye...after I shook off the pain...I was...amused.

Charlie attempts to retreat, wincing at the movement, and I am no longer amused.

I show her my teeth, and she freezes. Then I snap my mouth shut as her pain and fear turn to dismay. I raise one leg, placing my foot gently—so gently—on her chest. I must be careful not to damage the fragile two-leg.

She yelps as I slowly push her down, pinning her in place. I keep my claws sheathed, and then I lean down, attempting to ignore the way she trembles as I lick at her wounds.

Charlie is silent, her jaw set as she stares toward the entrance to my lair. But her blue eyes are shining with... water. *Tears*. The word floats into my mind. The sight of the saltwater dripping down her face makes me want to snarl as I gently stroke along her cuts and bruises.

She ignores me as I return my attention to her head. The sun is low in the sky when Maez reappears.

"She will need water," Maez tells me. Charlie ignores her, and I glare down at her. Betrayal. That's what the new scent is. She believes Maez should have helped her. Should have taken her from me.

The thought is ludicrous, and I step away, allowing Maez to approach with a cup of water. Now that the two-leg is no longer bleeding, I'm able to tolerate Maez as she hands Charlie the cup. Charlie gulps it down, and Maez leaves before returning when it is filled once more. She repeats this again until Charlie shakes her head at the offered cup.

The sun has set, and Charlie is shivering. I lie next to her, and she finally returns her attention to my face. I raise one wing over her, protecting her from the elements, and lay my head next to hers as I close my eyes.

Charlie

Someone is shining a light in my face. I scowl, attempting to raise a hand to shield my eyes. It's probably a cop, about to bang on my car window and tell me I can't sleep here.

I can't raise my arm, and panic makes me jolt awake. There's no cop, no car, and no Earth. I blink back tears as it all hits me again. I'm on Agron, on top of what appears to be a mountain, and the light is from the sun, which is rising on my left.

My arm is trapped by a huge wing. A dragon's wing. *Dragix,* I mouth, remembering what the purple woman called him yesterday. I gaze up at the sky, attempting to come to terms with the fresh hell I've woken up to.

Count your blessings, Charlie. You're alive, you're no longer stumbling through the woods, and the dragon hasn't barbecued you yet.

The dragon lets out a snore, and I stare as smoke twirls up above our heads. Now that he's not holding me down with his giant foot, I take the time to examine him.

His scales are warm. In fact, I'm so toasty beneath his wing that I'm almost sweating in spite of the slight chill of the morning.

He's so huge it seems unbelievable. His head is longer than my torso, and the claw I'm currently studying is larger than my hand. The rest of him is curled, almost like a cat, his huge body bunched as if ready to take off at any moment.

His scales aren't blue *or* green. They're both and every color in between. Some are such a light blue that they appear almost silver, while others are such a dark green that they're almost black.

Along that serpentine neck, sharp horns jut up, even more protection from anyone—or anything—that would be dumb enough to attack. Something swishes along the ground, and I crane my head, wondering if I need to be wary of snakes up here.

It's his tail. It sweeps lazily along the ground, and I return my attention to his face as he opens his mouth in a yawn, showcasing those gleaming rows of teeth.

On this planet, he's one-hundred-percent predator, and I'm nothing but prey.

But I've been outweighed and outmatched before and survived. This is no different.

I just need to figure out how to sneak away from this oversize lizard.

The lizard in question opens one eye, then the other, his gaze already on my face. I attempt to raise my arms again, and he shifts his wing. I instantly regret it as I lose the warmth, but he huddles close as we survey each other in silence.

I had a reason for telling him my name yesterday. On Earth, we're told that if we're ever kidnapped, we're supposed to attempt to build a relationship with our kidnapper. People are less likely to kill you when they see you as a human being.

I snort. Who knows if that will work on Agron.

Either way, if I can build some kind of bond with the dragon—who clearly understands me—maybe I can convince him to let me go.

My stomach chooses this moment to let out a growl.

Dragix's eyes widen, and he moves his head close to my

stomach, tilting his head as if waiting. He doesn't have long to wait, and a few seconds later, it lets out another howl.

His gaze returns to my face, and his eyes appear to be dancing with...amusement.

I scowl at him, and he casts me a warning look as he gets to his feet. He's so huge that I wonder how he doesn't accidentally squash me, but his feet are surprisingly nimble.

He steps back and scans our surroundings, lifting his head as he sniffs. He seems satisfied when he looks back at me. Then he glances toward the entrance to his lair. He steps toward it, and with a nudge of his nose, he pushes a huge boulder in front of the wide entranceway, blocking it off.

Then he crouches slightly before shooting into the sky. My mouth drops open. He removed my only way off this mountain.

"You son of a bitch!" I scream after him, attempting to ignore his answering roar.

It's a lot easier to yell at a dragon who is flying *away* from you.

My bladder is making itself known, and I get to my feet, cursing Dragix again for leaving me here. I walk to the side of the flat top of the mountain, my stomach twisting at the long drop down. Nothing but sheer rock. I walk around the perimeter anyway. There's no real trail, but on the far side, close to the entrance that Dragix just blocked off, I find a path that could work.

It would take some serious climbing skills to pull it off. I'd be inching down backward, clinging to the rock and hoping I didn't slip. But...if I could get down around ten feet, I could make my way along those rocks until I hit the bushes and trees further down.

From there, I would need to hoof it until I could find some way to hide my scent.

If Dragix is leaving me now, he may leave me again. Or maybe I can even sneak away when he's sleeping.

If he doesn't eat me first.

There are a few scant bushes to the right of the boulder that Dragix used to block off my preferred escape route. I crouch behind them and pee, cursing the dragon the whole time, and I'm pulling up the rags that used to be my pajama pants when I spot a dot in the distance.

A dot that's getting bigger.

Dragix lands with a *thump*, and I jolt as he places a dead creature on the ground in front of him, angling his head as he returns his attention to me. He raises one foot, the claws glinting at me in the sunlight, and gestures toward the animal—the movement somehow imperious.

I raise my middle finger and give him a gesture of my own.

He doesn't get the insult and simply stares at me. His gaze flicks between me and the poor dead animal in front of him.

My stomach growls again, and he narrows his eyes on me, his clawed foot jabbing at the animal once again.

"You're kidding, right?"

The growing annoyance in those gold eyes tells me that he is very much not kidding.

I survey the animal. It's furry, with four legs, not unlike a sheep or goat on Earth. It's also covered in blood, and my stomach roils as I gag.

Dragix seems exceedingly offended by this, his eyes widening with outrage and then narrowing again as he glances between me and the animal.

"That's greatly appreciated, but why don't you eat it instead?"

He steps closer, and I step back. Just like that, he's suddenly in front of me, clearing the top of the mountain in a single leap. His wing flies out, pulling me closer to him, and he bares his teeth at me as he flicks his eyes behind my shoulder. I glance back, realizing I just got way too close to the edge of the mountain.

"Uh, thanks. Great reflexes you've got there."

He ignores that, herding me back toward the dead animal with his wing. I dig my heels into the rock, wincing as the sharp edge of the stone cuts into my foot.

Dragix snarls at that, immediately lowering his head to lick at the wound.

"Are you a dragon or a mother hen?" I move my foot away, and he ignores me until he's finished with the licking.

Then he once again gestures at the bleeding carcass.

"I'm not hungry."

He roars. I stumble back from him as the sound leaves him, and a flame shoots from his mouth and into the air.

He's not the first male I've made roar with impatience, and unless he eats me, he won't be the last. But he's definitely the most terrifying, and my heart is thundering, my whole body shaking as I inch backward.

This time, I'm careful not to get too close to the side of the mountain. My eyes sting, and I wipe at them, frustrated, terrified, and just plain mad.

Dragix studies me, his tail lashing along the ground. The air still feels warm from the fire he spat out, although that might just be my imagination.

Wait. Fire.

"Hold on," I raise one hand. "Can you...cook that animal with your fire? I can't eat it raw. It'll make me sick."

He steps closer to the animal, blows out a breath, and sets it on fire.

I jump back, and he flicks me a glance, again warning me away from the edge of the mountain. I move forward again, and he returns his attention to the animal. The smell of burning hair, or...fur, turns my stomach, but it rumbles again at the underlying scent of cooking meat.

A few moments later, Dragix inhales deeply. I stare, stunned, as the flames flicker, die down, and then disappear completely.

Holy shit. Not only can he breathe fire, but he can put it out too. With just one inhalation.

He nods toward the animal, and I gingerly move closer. He seems impatient, almost desperate for me to eat, and I narrow my eyes at him. Maybe he's planning to fatten me up before he eats me?

I swallow as I stare at the animal, unsure where to start. Dragix raises one foot, and his claws swipe out. He makes quick work of skinning the animal and cutting off a large piece. Then he reaches his foot—or maybe it's a hand—out to me, and my mouth waters as the scent of cooked meat hits me.

I can't remember the last time I ate.

I reach out and take the meat. It's cooked through and surprisingly tender as I take a bite. It tastes slightly gamey, almost like rabbit, but I take another piece and then another, eating until there's no way my stomach could handle any more.

Dragix stares at me as I refuse the next piece of meat.

"Thank you," I tell him. "It was really good, but I'm full now. You should eat the rest."

He glances back at what's left of the animal. Guilt strikes me at how little I've eaten, but then I'm shuddering as

Dragix tears into it, polishing it off in two bites. He swallows the entire thing—bones and all—his teeth snapping shut when he's done.

Jesus, he's scary.

I have to get out of here because if he ever decides to turn those teeth on me...

My stomach roils as I stare at the spot where the animal was lying before meeting Dragix's gaze.

"Thanks again," I say, my voice shaking, and he turns, stalking away.

CHAPTER THREE

C harlie

I tremble. Not because I'm cold but because I'm slowly attempting to gather what's left of my courage.

It's dark, and Dragix has obviously decided that it's time to bed down for the night.

The day passed slowly. After we ate, Dragix pushed the boulder away from the huge entrance leading down into his mountain. I watched closely and could see the bob of the purple woman's head as she climbed a set of stairs.

She introduced herself as Maez and brought a wooden jug of water with the cup. When I'd drank my fill, she refilled the jug and left it behind.

I spent the day brooding, sitting in the shade of the huge boulder. Dragix ignored me for most of the day, flying off occasionally. But he was never gone for longer than what I estimated was ten minutes or so.

I have three options. The first is to wait here until he lets me go. But who knows when—or if—that'll happen. The next option is to learn to anticipate his schedule, picking the moment when he's likely to spend the most time away from this mountain to escape. Or I can try to sneak away when he's sleeping at night.

While he was gone, I examined my escape site, surveying the side of the mountain. I mentally climbed down a hundred times, picturing where I'd put my hands and feet as I scrambled down the rock.

It's going to be even more dangerous at night, but I have to go when he's sleeping. He's not leaving me much time with his quick trips to wherever he goes when he flies off this mountain. And only an idiot would stay here with a giant dragon.

The way his teeth snapped on whatever that animal was... I shiver. When he returned from his last excursion, he'd carried another animal with him. This time, he cut off raw pieces of the beast, holding them in the air with one foot while he breathed a steady stream of fire onto them. He then handed them to me to eat, and when I was completely full, he ate what was left of the animal.

Lesson: Dragix likes his food raw.

I bring my attention back to the present. This time, I was smart enough to make sure my arms were above the heavy wing Dragix laid over me.

My plan is simple. Roll away from him and head to my escape route. And don't make a fucking sound. Then run like hell. I go over the steps in my head until I'm trembling so hard that I'm worried my shaking will wake up Dragix.

I begin to inch out from under Dragix's wing. I close my eyes so that if he wakes, it'll hopefully look like I'm just turning in my sleep. But I'm suddenly so convinced that he's awake and watching me that I open my eyes to slits so I can see his face.

Eyes still closed. Good.

I have no chance of lifting his heavy wing off me without waking him. So I cross my left leg over my right, using my right arm to push against the ground as I roll myself over.

I make it onto my side and freeze.

Quiet as a mouse. Still. Silent.

But I'm not a mouse. Not any longer.

Never again.

I listen to Dragix's breathing for a few minutes and then roll again until I'm facedown. I repeat this twice more, cursing the sheer size of his wings. Finally, I'm lying beneath the very edge of his wing, and it's only covering half of my body.

When Dragix doesn't move, I make myself roll again. Otherwise, I'll lose my nerve. Yesterday—God, was it only yesterday?—when he brought me here, I was determined to make him angry enough that he'd eat me quickly. Now I'm terrified that this escape attempt will actually make that happen.

I roll once more, gently easing away from wing. I make myself stay lying on the ground, as if I've simply moved away in my sleep. Dragix doesn't wake, and I try to keep my breath even—attempting to ease the tightness in my chest.

I crouch, and then I slowly get to my feet.

I'm careful not to step on any stones, dried leaves, or anything else that could give me away. I scan my surroundings, daring a glance back at Dragix. I study the large entryway where Maez disappears to, but I have no idea what's waiting for me down there.

Better the devil I know.

I gauge the distance to the side of the mountain. If I thought Dragix wouldn't be able to catch me, I'd run toward it. But I've seen how quickly he can move. My best chance is to creep quietly. Like a mouse.

Not a mouse. Not anymore.

Dragix lets out a snore, and I jump slightly. Then I slowly creep toward my path back to the other women and hopefully back to Earth.

I have no idea how I'm going to get down the side of the mountain without alerting the predator at my back.

Cross that bridge when you come to it.

I tiptoe toward the side of the mountain. Dragix stops snoring, and I glance back over my shoulder. In the darkness, his scales glimmer in the moonlight, and his eyes gleam like melted gold as he opens them and glares straight at me.

Fear slams into me like a freight train. I'm suddenly that mouse again, sizing up my chance of surviving the cat that's slowly getting to its feet.

I run.

I know I shouldn't. Predators love it when you run. When you show you're scared. But I can't help it. I bolt to the side of the mountain and scramble down, hauling myself over the rock until only my hands are holding on to the rock above me.

Dragix lets out a roar that makes the mountain tremble.

If I weren't holding on to the rock for dear life, slipping and sliding my way down the side of the mountain, I'd slap my hands over my ears.

Instead, I scream back. My scream is half rage, half pure, undiluted terror.

A gust of air hits my face, and I move faster, my bare feet sliding for purchase on the rock. The sound of flapping wings turns my panicked breaths into dry sobs, and then I'm snatched up once again, Dragix pulling me away from the mountain and into the sky as the air turns hot with his rage.

He roars at me again, and this time I do slap my hands over my ears as he drops me back on the top of the mountain.

"Fuck you!" I scream back.

He throws his head with a snarl, baring those lethally sharp teeth at me, and then he seems to turn into a burst of light.

My mouth drops open. I'm looking at a man.

A man who looks as surprised as I am.

He's butt naked, bronze skin gleaming in the moonlight. His hair falls beneath his shoulders, tousled and as gold as his eyes, which widen as he brings one of his hands up to his face.

He takes a step and stumbles, staring down at his feet as if confused.

I rub at my eyes.

A dragon was bad enough. This proves that I'm truly going insane. Am I even on an alien planet? Or did I have some kind of breakdown and I'm really on Earth, about to wake up from a nightmare?

Silence stretches between us as he stares at me. I carefully—very carefully—avoid dropping my gaze any lower.

Butt. Naked.

He looks like a Greek god, and he seems to have figured out how his body works because he stalks toward me. He's still relatively unsteady on his feet, but his face turns hard as he frowns at me.

"You will not leave."

My eyes widen. Thanks to the Arcav, I have a translator in my ear. But the dragon...

"You speak my language?"

He gives me a look. "My people speak all languages," he says. His voice is low and rough, and his mouth seems to hesitate as he forms the words, but his tone drips with arrogance.

Of course they do. Why wouldn't they?

If he understands me, maybe we can talk this out.

"Look, I get that you're used to being the ruler of the animal kingdom around here. But if you're not planning to eat me—and I really hope you're not—then please let me go."

For some unknown reason, he seems surprised by my request. His thick brows rise, his gold eyes widen, and then he scowls at me, as if the very suggestion is ludicrous.

"I am tired of being alone," he says. "I have healed you, fed you, and kept you safe. You will stay here until I decide you may leave."

I clench my teeth so hard I'm surprised they don't crack.

Not only is he both a dragon and a man—and how the hell is that even possible?—but he's clearly crazy.

"You're not alone. You have Maez."

He ignores that, seemingly distracted by one of his fingers, which he holds up in front of his face, studying it with a frown.

"Yo," I interrupt the staring. "Did you hear me? I want to leave. You can't keep me here."

He meets my gaze. "I saw you, and I took you. I am Dragix. I can do what I like."

For some reason, I attract crazy like honey attracts bees on Earth. This planet is obviously going to be no different. I open my mouth, and he narrows his eyes at me.

"I am faster than you and stronger than you, even in this form. You cannot leave."

With that, he turns back into a dragon, effectively ending our conversation.

***

Dragix

I had...forgotten my two-leg form. It has been so many centuries since I chose to walk instead of fly that the shift took me by surprise. From the look of wrath on Charlie's face as she stares back at me, she is not pleased by my shift back to my dragon form.

It was entirely unplanned.

For the first time in longer than I can remember, a shadow of fear slides over me.

I am shifting forms with no warning.

What if I shift back to my two-leg form while flying with Charlie?

No. I will not take her off this mountain until I have remembered how to control the shift.

I gesture toward the ground where we sleep, and Charlie stalks toward it, her back straight, her shoulders tight. Now that I have felt the rough ground beneath my bare feet, I realize that it cannot be comfortable for her to sleep on.

I felt the little two-leg remaining tense and awake next to me even as she pretended she was sleeping. So I also feigned sleep, wondering just how she would attempt to escape.

She has no understanding of how sensitive I am to movement, noise, and smell. Even if I had been in a deep sleep, I would have woken as she rolled away from me.

I didn't expect her to attempt to scramble down the side of my mountain. I thought she would go deeper into my lair, where she would likely have become lost and I would have easily trailed her scent.

Instead, she could have lost her life. Her short two-leg life. I rustle my wings at the thought, and Charlie shifts next to me. She is not sleeping and is instead staring up at the night sky, her jaw tight as she ignores me.

My two-leg form. I had forgotten. Forgotten that my people had this form even though we once used it just as much as our winged form. We danced in this form, laughed in this form, mated in this form. My parents...

No.

I push away the thought. If my people had spent more time in their winged form, perhaps they would still be alive today.

I smell salt and glance at Charlie. Tears are tracking silently down her face as she looks up at the stars. She sniffs, and something in my chest hurts.

I harden myself against it. I am Dragix. Two-leg tears mean nothing to me.

Charlie

I don't bother getting up the next morning.

There's no point. Instead, I ignore Dragix as he rises, and I push his head away as he snuffles at me. He may think he's won, but I can outlast him. Three years ago, I promised myself that I'd never be a prisoner again.

And I keep my promises.

Dragix stomps away, his tail flicking over the ground as he lets out a sound somewhere between a hiss and a growl.

Oh, I'm sorry, is your pet not entertaining you as much as you'd like? Maybe you should let her fucking go.

On the bright side, I'm not living in constant terror now. If he was going to kill and eat me, he likely would've done it last night, when the air around us heated with his rage.

Dragix must turn back to me because I can feel those gold eyes on my face. I ignore him, and he stomps in my direction. He waits until I eventually meet his gaze and then shows me the edges of his teeth.

Asshole.

"What do you want?"

He obviously can't reply, and this pleases me. Frustration shines in those gleaming eyes, and then he leans down, pushing against me with his head.

He wants me to get up.

"Sorry, I don't speak giant lizard. Maybe you should turn back into a man and we can have an actual conversation."

He roars at me, and I slap my hands over my ears.

Then, with a gust of air, he takes off, shooting up into the sky in the blink of an eye.

God, he's fast.

Now that he's gone, I drag myself to my feet. Maez will likely come up soon. Maybe I can take her by surprise and knock her out. Then I can skedaddle down into the mountain and haul ass out of here before Dragix gets back.

Except that she never comes up here unless he's here, and he rolled that godforsaken rock in front of those stairs last night. All while staring at me as if to say "go ahead and move that."

I move back to my shady spot but leave my legs in the sun as the day heats. I'm not used to Dragix being gone for so long. Usually, I'd estimate it at less than twenty minutes, but the sun is rising in the sky, and he's still not back.

Am I missing a perfectly good opportunity to escape? Or maybe he's punishing me? Perhaps he has even decided to just leave me here to rot.

I get to my feet and walk the perimeter. Again. In the distance, the calls of birds sound, followed by a howl that gives me goose bumps. Misty, early-morning sunlight softens the plains in front of me. To my right, a forest stretches, and through the green leaves, I can see dark-blue branches reaching for the sky.

A herd of the animals that Dragix seems to love are moving as one across a wide meadow on my left, and I can practically hear the thunder of their hooves as they sprint for the cover of the trees.

Likely because they're aware of the huge predator who likes to pick them off whenever he wants a snack.

It still feels weird to be looking up at a green sky, and I'm suddenly so incredibly homesick that I'm once again brushing tears off my cheeks.

Earth wasn't perfect, that's for sure. Especially for me. Sleeping in my car wasn't exactly a good time, and moving from state to state to escape my sociopath ex was wearing on me. Never being able to make friends, only working temp jobs—it sucked. Not to mention, I was abducted by the Grivath on Earth. Being sold on an alien planet and crash-landing on this one? Also not cool.

But living in my car was better than this.

Finally, finally, Dragix approaches. I stay seated in the shade as he lands, his gaze going straight to me.

Then that bright light comes out of nowhere and he's suddenly a man again. Only this time, he looks much more comfortable in his body as he stalks toward me.

I stand up, if only to avoid looking up at his giant—

Don't think about that. Do not. Think. About. That.

"Where have you been?" I snap. "If you're going to keep me here, you can't just take off and leave me without any water."

He nods. "You are right. I apologize."

I'm so stunned to hear those words from the guy that I blink, almost missing what he says next.

"I have been practicing my shift," he says. He steps back, transforms into a dragon and then back again.

This time, it's *his* stomach that rumbles, and the corner of his mouth tips up.

He's beautiful. So incredibly beautiful that it almost hurts to look at him. But he's also a dragon, and he's keeping me here against my will.

"Shifting forms quickly drains my energy and makes me hungry. If I do not eat, I will not be able to spit flame," he explains as if I asked.

"I need to get off this mountain." My words are weary, no longer pleading. I'll keep saying them until he lets me go, even if I don't expect that to happen anytime soon.

Shock hits me when he nods.

"You're letting me go?"

One firm shake of his head, and I turn away, unable to even look at him.

His hand is firm and warm—so warm—on my shoulder when he spins me back around.

"I know you are upset. I would not want to be trapped without wings. I will take you with me while I hunt."

"Really?"

He nods and raises one eyebrow expectantly.

It burns. Burns to have to thank this motherfucker for "allowing" me off this mountain.

But I'll play the game until he lets down his guard enough for me to sneak away.

"Thank you," I say, forcing out the words. He inclines his head, and then suddenly he's a dragon again, and the gurgle of his stomach sounds like a roar.

CHAPTER FOUR

C harlie

Once again, I'm flying, cupped in a dragon's hand. Or foot. Maybe I should ask Dragix about that next time he's in his man form.

It's certainly not a human form. No matter which form it takes, it's clear from the gold of his eyes, the shadow of scales over his body, and the way he speaks that he is one-hundred-percent alien.

I close my eyes briefly as Dragix banks left, and I get an up-close look at the tops of some of Agron's tallest trees. Earlier, he snatched up some kind of animal from a herd— the injured one that was failing to keep up with the others, surprise, surprise—and shoved the whole thing in his mouth.

I covered my ears in an attempt to drown out the crunch of the bones, and Dragix narrowed one gold eye at me.

Now he's eyeing up another herd of animals as we fly over a giant, grassy field.

"Please," I yell up at him, the wind stealing my words, but I know he can hear me when he raises me closer to his head. "If you're going to hunt, can you put me down somewhere first? You're making me queasy."

Dragix seems to consider it, glancing down at the animals. Then he lets out a sigh, and I squeal, slamming my eyes shut as he folds in his wings and arrows toward the ground.

His chest rumbles. Is he...laughing?

He lands with a thump, and I open my eyes, almost kissing the ground when he places me on it.

He's standing naked in front of me a moment later, and I step forward as he moves closer.

"What are you—hey!"

He casually reaches for me, pulling me toward him, and I clench my hand into a fist. He gives me a warning look and then leans forward, sniffing at my hair.

One long inhale, and then he steps back.

"Did you just...sniff me?"

"I ensured that I have your scent, two-leg. If you run from me, I will find you. And I will not let you out of my sight again."

I grind my teeth, pointing to the river in the distance. "I want to sit by the water. Is that okay with Your Majesty?"

He nods. "I won't be long."

Then he shifts and he's gone. He flies even faster when I'm not with him, and I don't quite know what to make of that.

I head toward the water. God, I need a bath. When I woke up on top of that mountain, there was a lot less blood on my body, but my pajamas are still covered in rust-colored stains, and I must smell ripe.

I glance around me, but I'm completely alone. Dragix likely scanned this place before he landed, using that incredible nose of his to check no one else was around.

In that case...

I stare down at my filthy body and raise a hand to my hair, which is still stiff with blood.

That's it. I'm going in.

I glance up at the sky one more time, but Dragix is nowhere to be found. So I strip. I dump my pajamas on the ground and stride straight into the water, careful of the sharp stones beneath my feet. The stones give way to sand, and I don't let myself think about the scary, likely poisonous alien creatures that could be waiting below.

I dunk myself, gasping as I rise out of the water. The water is freezing, and the shade from the trees overhead isn't helping. Later on in the day, when the heat of the sun is beaming down, this water would be an excellent way to cool off.

I grab some sand and use it to scour my body. Then I dunk my head, scrubbing at my scalp. No shampoo, but even a rinse is better than nothing. I'm shivering as I throw my head back and turn to find Dragix landing next to the river, his eyes wider than I've ever seen them.

"Turn around!" I snap, and surprisingly, he does. My teeth are clattering as I wring out my hair before I reach for my pajamas. I really, really don't want to put them back on, but it's either that or hang out naked, and that's not an option.

Dragix doesn't bother changing form, simply scoops up my shivering body and takes to the skies.

The day is heating up, and Dragix is holding me in the perfect position for the sun to warm my body as we fly.

It's...kind. In fact, I have to admit that most of the things he has done so far have been kind—healing me, making sure I had water, hunting food and then cooking it for me. Not to mention keeping me warm under his wing at night. Unfortunately, they don't negate the fact that he hasn't yet been convinced to let me go and rejoin the other women.

Dragix swoops down, and I slam my eyes shut as he casually kills another beast, holding it tight with his claws. I'm guessing that's my lunch.

What if the other women who were taken have already figured out how to get off this planet? What if they've been waiting for me and they're eventually going to leave without me?

We were all taken together, but really, we don't owe each other anything. If they get a chance to go back to Earth, will they take it and leave me here?

Dragix lands on our mountain. *His* mountain. And we do the whole cook, eat, try not to puke when the dragon crunches down on the rest of the poor animal routine.

Then he pushes aside the boulder, and I expect to see Maez waiting. Instead, he shifts back into a man and steps toward the stairs, gesturing for me to follow him.

Is this a trick?

Obviously not because Dragix is casting an impatient look over his shoulder. I jump into action and follow him into his lair.

The staircase is steep, but there are torches placed along the walls, the dancing flames providing enough light to ensure I don't tumble down the stairs.

And down we go. I don't know what I expected, but it

wasn't a spiral staircase leading to a small landing with a few doors, followed by another staircase and then another.

It's dark. But strangely, the tall ceilings and the fresh air I can feel wafting in from somewhere ensure that it's not claustrophobic. I guess if you're a winged creature choosing to live inside, you're going to make sure you don't feel trapped.

The walls are mostly smooth rock, and this whole place seems...ancient.

How the hell did so much of this mountain get cut away without risking the structural integrity?

I can hear running water somewhere, and I'm instantly ready to explore this place and discover its secrets. But Dragix pauses before we go down yet another set of stairs and again gestures for me to follow him—this time into a room. I blink, realizing that the dirt and stone has been removed to reveal a window overlooking a shady forest.

A collection of wooden chests is sitting near the window, and I avert my eyes from Dragix's ridiculously toned butt as he leans down and opens one of them. He's not at all self-conscious about his nudity—and why would he be with that body?—but I'm still attempting to ignore the way my traitorous hormones react to all that golden skin.

Since I'm keeping my eyes on the stone wall, and carefully *not* fantasizing about what it would feel like to have that huge body wrapped around mine, it takes me a moment to realize Dragix is saying my name.

I glance back at him in time to see his nostrils flare as his eyes scan my body, lingering on my hardened nipples.

Please tell me he can't smell my arousal.

From the way his eyes have darkened, I'd say he sure can.

I clear my throat and reach for the bundle of clothes he's holding out.

"These were my sister's," he says, and his eyes are no longer dark with what might have been his own lust. No, they're dark with pain, his expression bleak for an instant before his face hardens again.

I'm guessing his sister isn't here anymore.

"Thank you," I murmur. "I appreciate it."

He nods, and instead of leaving me to get changed, once again gestures for me to follow him.

We travel down several more flights of stairs, and then this time, the landing drops off. I step closer to the edge, peering over the stone.

Whoa.

The walkway I'm standing on is wrapped around the inside of the mountain, and it spirals down, with open doorways on every level. What I thought was his entire lair is really just one wing of it.

"This place is massive."

Dragix nods. "It was once home to my people. All of them."

His eyes are shuttered as he turns away, and as much as I want to ask what the hell happened to those people, I don't.

Silence stretches between us as Dragix leads me down one more flight of stairs. Then I'm blinking in shock as he steps aside. Several pools are cut into the side of the mountain, steam rising into the air.

"No way," I murmur. The hint of a smile is playing around his mouth when I glance at him.

"You will likely enjoy this more than the river."

I angle my head. "You didn't think to tell me that there were hot pools down here?"

"You didn't ask."

Funny guy.

"Why did you keep me upstairs on the top of the mountain?"

"I am too big to navigate this place in my full form."

I stare at him, and his jaw tightens.

"I had forgotten that I could shift," he admits, turning away.

Wow. When he said he was practicing, I thought he was rusty—not that he'd just straight up forgotten that he used to walk around as a man. No wonder he examined his hand like he'd never seen before. It also explains why he seemed so unsteady on his feet when he first shifted.

"I will send Maez with the things you need."

"Thank you," I say, and this time, it's easier to say the words without choking. He didn't have to do this. He saw me freezing my butt off in the river and realized I needed a proper bath.

He simply nods and walks away.

Dragix

I am...different in this form. When I have two legs instead of four, the memories come like a wave. Being down here, in the place that was once home, makes it worse.

There, by the window, is where my sister used to sit and gaze out at the world. She could daydream for hours, days, but she always had a smile for anyone who interrupted her quiet time.

And in this place, there were always interruptions.

Our home was thriving, packed with our families, living together, mating, laughing. Near the end, there was no laughter, simply silence, tears, mourning as we buried what was left of our people.

It's the younglings that I think of in this form. The way they would scamper through this place, shifting from two-leg to winged form and eventually falling down in a heap, exhausted as they forgot to eat. They'd be picked up and cuddled by whoever walked by and taken back to their parents for food and rest.

We were happy here.

In this form, it's more difficult to stand by my decision to keep Charlie with me. Logic wars with instinct.

What if she has family on this planet? Someone who misses her? A...mate? My blood heats at the thought as I stalk through my lair, looking for Maez.

But no...I have not seen two-legs like Charlie on this planet. Small, with pale-colored skin and no claws, fangs, or scales. She is...different.

I will ask her at the first opportunity.

I have been good to the female two-leg. I have kept her safe. Without me, she would die on this planet. She may not want to be here, but she will stay.

I will protect her, and she will keep my loneliness at bay.

CHAPTER FIVE

C harlie

Time passes. Now that Dragix can switch between forms, he takes me down into the lair whenever I like. I spend hours relaxing in the hot pools, while he disappears to do who knows what.

We haven't spoken about his family, but now that he's remembered what he refers to as his "two-leg form," he spends more time in it. He often wanders through the huge rabbit warren inside this mountain for hours, his expression lost.

Maez has made herself scarce. She ensures I have everything I need—including soap, a comb, and even long strips of clean material cut into pieces for when my period arrives.

Dragix has given me what used to be his sister's room, so I tuck my makeshift pads into one of the huge wooden chests that passes for my closet. I stroke my hand over it, wondering about the woman who used to live in this room, who slept in the large bed in the corner. Dragix seems to realize that sleeping on the hard ground on top of the mountain isn't exactly my preference, so he allows me to sleep down here instead.

During the day, I'll often find him snoozing on the top of his mountain, his scales gleaming like fire in the sunlight. But at night, he refuses to leave me down here alone, choosing instead to sleep in what must have been a huge communal area at the bottom of the mountain. If I leave my room and peek over the side of the stone walkway, I can see him curled up like a cat, far below me.

I haven't tried to escape yet. I'm smart enough to bide my time. I've done it before.

I push away the memories of Ben and climb the stairs to find Dragix.

I'm...bored.

I've been here for days, and I'm no closer to convincing Dragix to let me see the other women. But if I can just get a glimpse of them, they'll at least know I'm alive. Then, maybe, they'll think twice before they leave without me.

If they even *can* leave.

From what I've gathered so far, we may be trapped here. I've seen no planes, no cars, nothing that would suggest that the people here know how to travel through space. The ship we landed in... I have no idea if we'd be able to use it to leave.

The thought is depressing, but I shake it off. This is just one part of this planet. Who knows what else Agron has to offer? Maybe this area is like the Amazon rain forest on Earth, and there could even be a New York City that I just haven't seen yet.

I snort. Right.

Dragix gets to his feet as soon as I make it up the stairs. The sun beats down on us, warming my skin, but at least up here there is a breeze to counter the sweltering heat.

"What is wrong?"

"Holy shit! You can speak in my *mind?* How long were you going to keep that on the down low for?"

Dragix ignores me, his tail swishing along the ground as he stalks closer.

"You are bleeding. Tell me why."

If the mountain opened up and swallowed me whole, it would be preferable to this.

Of course he can smell my blood. He's the king of predators.

"Um."

He steps closer, his nostrils flaring, and then I squeak, pushing his head away as he sniffs at my hair, neck, and then lower.

"It's my period, Dragix. Get a grip!"

He angles his head, staring at me.

"My uh...cycle. And if you could not let me know that you can *smell* it, that would be great."

If I didn't know better, I would think the dragon was embarrassed with the way he backs away, his tail lying like a dead snake on the ground.

Change the subject. For the love of God, change the subject.

"You can talk in my head? Can you read my mind as well?" No wonder he was pretending to sleep that night when I tried to escape.

"No. I am able to open a pathway to your mind, allowing for conversation. You are able to speak back. I had...forgotten. It was only when I thought you were hurt and needed to know where

that I remembered I could still communicate. It happened auto-matically."

He refuses to look at me. It must be difficult to admit that he's basically forgotten who and what he is. Something aches in my chest with the need to make him feel better.

"LIKE THIS?" I shoot the words at him like bullets from a gun, unsure how much force to put behind them. I'm squinting at his head, and from the low rumble that comes from Dragix's throat, I obviously look constipated.

"Quieter." His voice is a low murmur. Soft. Intimate. *"You are yelling."*

Oops. He no longer looks like he's about to settle into a long brood though. Although why I should care is beyond me.

"Listen," I say aloud. "I'm bored. How about we go for a flight? I'd love to see the spaceship that I crash-landed in."

He narrows his eyes slightly on my face, and I keep it—and my mind—carefully blank. He could be lying about being able to read my thoughts.

And I'm desperately hoping that the other women will be hanging out near that ship.

After a long pause, Dragix nods. He holds out his foot, claws gleaming like polished obsidian, and I sigh.

"You do not wish to go?"

"I do. It's just...it feels a little weird being carried around by a dragon."

"Weird?"

I attempt to send a mental picture down the pathway. My eyes are squeezed almost shut as I stare at Dragix's head, and he snorts.

I ignore his obvious amusement. Not all of us are used to talking with our minds.

Those gold eyes widen and then narrow on my face, and

I know he's picked up the image of Godzilla with a person clutched in one hand and a car clutched in the other.

"This creature is not of this world."

I laugh. "It's not of any worlds. It's made up."

He blinks. Twice.

I wave a hand. "Let's not go into that now. Anyway, it's fine; let's just go."

I walk toward him, the breeze rustling my hair. He's silent for a long moment, and then he moves his foot away.

My heart sinks. I really, *really* wanted to fly. Now that I have a pretty good feeling Dragix isn't going to drop me for funsies, I think I'd actually be able to enjoy it this time.

For some weird reason, I trust the guy—dragon—not to hurt me.

For now.

"You may ride on my back."

My eyebrows shoot up. "Seriously?"

He nods, and from the look in his eyes, the fact that he's allowing me to sit up there is a pretty big deal.

"Are you sure?"

"Get on my back before I change my mind."

I burst out laughing. That's the closest that Dragix has come to sounding almost...human.

But he's not human. And his ideas about personal freedom are probably the least human thing about him.

I can't forget that.

He offers his foot again, and this time, he holds it up to his shoulder.

I scramble up onto his back, careful not to impale myself with the horns along the back of his neck.

"Okay, maybe I was overly confident about this."

Dragix snorts again, a curl of smoke rising toward me. Then he gets to his feet, and I clutch uselessly at the horns.

I wrap my legs around him—in the spot where his shoulders meet his neck.

"Wait," I blurt. "This was a bad idea."

That rumble sounds again, and then I'm shrieking, screaming, hollering curses at the dragon as he shoots into the sky like a torpedo.

"You motherfuckerrrrrrrr." The wind steals my words, but I know Dragix can hear me from the way his shoulders shake. I switch to our mental pathway.

"I changed my mind. I changed it, Dragix. Go back!"

"You are fine. I will not let you fall. Relax and enjoy the ride."

Dragon humor.

"I'm not fine! I feel like I could slip off at any second." He banks right, and I curse, holding on to his horns for dear life. *"This isn't funny, Dragix!"*

"If you fall, I will catch you. Enjoy this moment, Charlie. Never have I allowed another two-leg to sit where you are."

I blink at that. *"Never?"*

He flaps his wings once and then ducks his head, angling us slightly downward. I can feel when we hit a warm current, and he keeps his wings spread, gliding through the air.

"Never has a two-leg ridden any dragon on this planet. You are the first."

Well, hot damn.

I don't know what to say to that, so I clutch his horns tighter and blow out a long breath. Now that he's not shooting into the sky or tilting his body so far that I feel like I'll roll off, I can actually lift my head.

My eyes stream, but it's worth it. It's more than worth it for the way the clouds part for us, for the way Dragix slowly angles downward until I can see the tops of trees. It's a completely different experience sitting on his back. It feels almost like I'm flying myself, and I can't help the delighted laugh that escapes my chest.

If I get off this planet and back to Earth, I'll be returning to a life of living in my car and picking up waitressing jobs as I move from city to city, state to state. That's if my car hasn't already been impounded. Riding a dragon? This may be the most exciting thing I ever do in my life. When I'm once again tying an apron around my waist in time for the second part of my split shift, I can think back to this moment.

So I open my eyes, and I lean forward—still clutching onto Dragix's horns for dear life. But I bask in the wonder as the wind snatches at my hair, my eyes drip tears down my cheeks, and I shoot through the sky on the back of a dragon.

Dragix

Never did I imagine that I would allow a two-leg to ride me the way that the Braxians ride their beasts. But where *this* two-leg is concerned, I find myself bending my own rules.

Her laugh of wonder earlier...it was reward enough for the breaking of my people's traditions.

I think that if my mother met this two-leg...if she saw the inner fire that makes all Charlie's moments burn with intensity...she would forgive me.

I stretch my right wing downward, and this time, Charlie lets out a delighted whoop behind me.

If I were in two-leg form, I might smile at that. And it has been a very long time since I have had the urge to smile.

I tuck my wings close, arrowing down toward the trees below us as Charlie shrieks. Then, at the last possible second, I open my wings once more, and we shoot back up into the sky.

"*You—you...*"

Charlie's voice trails off as I check that she is holding tight. Her legs are clamped around me, her hands clutching at my horns.

So I roll.

We're only upside down for a moment, and a scream rips from her throat. When we're soaring again, she growls behind me.

"You asshole!" A long silence. "Do it again!"

My urge to smile has deepened into an urge to laugh as I comply, and she screams again but also roars with laughter as we once again turn upright.

I am...showing off for her. And I'm not quite certain why.

All I know is that the sound of her laugh, the feel of her legs wrapped around me, the trust she has shown me...

I want more.

For once, we are not enemies. She is not my captive, planning her escape. And I am not the wicked creature refusing to allow her to leave.

Charlie gasps behind me.

"*There it is,*" she says, and I glance down. "*Can we get closer?*"

I angle down, circling until the metal is clear through the trees.

"*How did this happen?*" I ask.

A long silence. Her legs tighten further, as if the thought is one that scares her, and my blood heats once again.

"*I was living my life on Earth. We all were. Then I woke up on a ship. We were taken to a strange planet, where aliens bid on us like we were objects. Once we were sold, we were loaded on that ship. But the ship crashed, and the Voildi said they would help us. A group of massive guys jumped out at us, and I went looking for water. Then you found me."*

Her voice is sad.

"The Voildi...these are the yellow ones?"

"Yes."

"They were not helping you. They prefer their meat to be able to talk."

Charlie growls again behind me. *"Those assholes were going to eat us?"*

"Yes."

"Well, shit. Oh my God. What if the other women have been eaten?"

"The other males. What did they look like?"

"Um. I didn't pay much attention. They were huge though. They had long hair—like yours but darker. And they carried swords."

"Braxians." My voice is a hiss of rage, and Charlie jolts behind me as I search for a place to land.

"Is that bad? Do you think they hurt the other women?"

"No," I admit. *"They likely will be hoping to mate with them."*

"Oh God."

Charlie trembles against me. I choose not to tell her that the Braxians are unlikely to mate with her friends without permission. They may be barbarians, but they have their own code of honor.

A code of honor that didn't apply to my people.

I bare my teeth at the thought. Charlie is safer with me than with the traitorous Braxians. Let her believe that they would harm her if it makes her appreciate the safety she finds in my lair.

I land and help Charlie dismount. She glances up at me and then takes a step toward the twisted metal in front of us.

Her eyes scan our surroundings, and I can sense her disappointment. Ah. The other females. She was hoping that they would be here.

I grit my teeth as I transform into my two-leg form.

"What are you doing?" she asks.

"If you are planning to go inside, I must be in this form to go with you."

She stares at the ship, and for the first time in days, I can smell the reek of her terror.

I didn't notice when Charlie no longer smelled of fear and anxiety. Now she is trembling once more, and I mentally curse myself for bringing her back here.

She takes a few steps closer and then freezes, shaking her head.

"No," she says. "I'm not."

We're mostly silent on the way back, and I swoop down occasionally to hunt along the way. Now that I am changing between forms, I need more fuel than I can ever remember needing before.

I can feel Charlie flinch as I pick off a beast from the back of its herd.

"What is the matter?"

"Nothing. I was just remembering following the Voildi with the other women. I was the sick, injured human at the back of the herd. I kept thinking that it was only a matter of time before I was picked off by a predator."

I flinch internally at that. I was the predator who took her.

"Charlie—"

"It's okay, Dragix. It's the way the universe works. The weak are always the first to die. It's for the good of the herd. If predators

targeted the healthiest animals or the youngest, whole species would die out."

I turn my head to see her staring down at her hands, at where they're clenched tight around two of my horns.

"I didn't take you because you were the weakest. I took you because you smelled like something I hadn't smelled in centuries."

She looks up at that, meeting my eyes, and I return my attention to our flight, angling us back toward the mountain.

"What did I smell like?"

I'm silent for a long moment. *"You smelled like home."*

She says nothing until I land and shift into my two-leg form. Now that I have seen how much Charlie has enjoyed the heated water in my lair, I have decided to try it myself.

"Dragix?"

"Yes?"

She chews on her lip, and I have a sudden, strange desire to replace her teeth with mine, nipping at her soft mouth and soothing with my tongue.

I step away.

"Do you think the other women are okay?"

I study her face. I could lie to her now. Could tell her that the other female two-legs are likely scared. Perhaps even hurt. I could let her think that she was the lucky one. That I am her light in the darkness. That on a planet full of monsters, she was taken by the one least likely to kill her.

But her anxiety is still wafting toward me, and she has a line between her eyes as she gazes toward the ship. If I lie to her and allow her to believe that her friends are in grave peril, I will be the worst type of monster.

"No," I grit out. "Braxian males do not hurt females."

Her eyes widen, the anxiety replaced with a hint of hope. I like this scent better, I decide. I like her eyes on me, large and trusting. Even if it means that she will likely be more determined to return to those females.

"Really?"

"Yes."

Nothing has changed. She may wish to leave, but she cannot leave me. Strangely, the thought does not soothe me as I stalk away to bathe.

CHAPTER SIX

C harlie

I fly with Dragix almost every day. Sometimes, he points out different types of animals or tells me a little about the history of this planet. Other times, we fly in silence. When he's behaving—and not performing barrel rolls in the air—I occasionally take my hands from his horns, raising them high as I tip back my head, my grin so wide that my cheeks hurt.

Now that I know that the other women are okay—Dragix insisted that the Braxians would have easily killed the Voildi and taken the women back to their camp—I feel much more relaxed.

Oh, I'm still planning to escape when Dragix lets his guard down. But from the look of that ship, the other women can't go anywhere yet. For the first time in years, I'm not taking as many waitressing shifts as I can. I'm not hoarding money and wearing clothes that are little more than rags so that I'll be able to afford gas and maybe a motel next time I move. I'm not deliberating whether to eat a meal now or save that money to put toward my emergency fund so I can run the next time Ben finds me.

Dragix makes sure that I have more than enough food. When I explained to him that I can't live off meat and meat alone, he took me to Maez's small vegetable patch and then showed me which trees in the forest had the sweetest fruit.

Here, I can sleep for as long as I like, without the fear of someone tapping on my window—either ordering me to move my car or seeing me as their next victim.

The other women...they probably have real lives on Earth. Lives with careers and families.

Me? I have no one. Nothing. I know I can't stay on Agron forever. But for now, when I know that the other women aren't going anywhere without me?

I'm being selfish. I'm in no hurry to find the other women, to help them figure out how to get off this planet. To be fair, Dragix watches me constantly, and when he's not watching me, Maez is. I have such a small chance of escaping that I haven't even tried yet. And while I may feel that small trickle of guilt, I'm enjoying hanging out in Dragix's lair.

"What are they?" I return my attention to our flight.

Dragix glances down at the furry creatures below us.

"They know better than to come into my territory. They are Zintas, and they believe they can kill me, take my scales, and sell them."

Wait. What?

"You're being hunted?"

Dragix turns his head. *"My people have always been hunted."*

Who would be stupid enough to hunt a dragon?

Although, since Dragix is now living without his family, I'm guessing that at least some of those assholes were successful.

Dragix turns, then he jolts, and a roar leaves him.

"What is it?" I scream, and then I see it.

The Zintas are shooting at us. And one of them just hit us, an arrow sliding straight through Dragix's wing.

Oh God. *"Are we going down?"*

A snort. And then he deftly shifts to the side as another arrow flies past.

"Let's get out of here, Dragix."

"No. Their arrows could have killed you. I am going to show them the error of their ways."

"Huh?"

Dragix turns, and I get a better look at the Zintas. There are so many of them. All I can tell from up here is that they're bulky and furry as bears.

Dragix lets out another roar of retribution, and then I hold on tight as he tucks his wings close, heading toward the forest.

"Dragix. Dragix. Dragix!"

Oh God, we're going so fast. I know he's trying to make us a smaller target, but what if we crash?

I should've known better. He lands in a clearing so small the tree branches almost brush his wings as he opens them to slow our flight.

It's a rough landing, and I almost fall. But Dragix snatches me off his back, already crouching.

"Run," he says. *"I will find you, but you need to run."*

I swallow. Half of me wants to beg him to take me back to the mountain. But I get it. They came for him in a pack and attempted to shoot him out of the sky. They're in his territory. If he doesn't take care of the problem now, they'll think they won. They might bring more people next time, might come deeper into his territory.

The thought of his huge body falling from the sky makes my stomach twist, so I nod.

"I'm going," I say as he tilts his head impatiently. When I turn, a gust of wind hits me as he shoots up into the sky.

I almost feel sorry for the Zintas.

But he's right. If they saw where he landed, they could head toward me.

I bolt through the forest so fast that I'm almost flying. As worried as I am for Dragix, now that he doesn't need to protect me, he can sure as hell handle himself.

And if a dragon tells you to run...you run.

I jump over tree branches, crying out as I land on a sharp rock. I've been walking around the lair barefoot, and I forgot to check if Dragix's sister's shoes would fit me.

Idiot.

I sprint until I'm so out of breath that I'm forced to stop, and then I lean over, hands on my knees as I suck in air. I have no idea where I am, no idea where Dragix is, but I can hear water pounding against rocks somewhere close by.

Once I catch my breath, I head toward it. Dragix made it clear that he has my scent that first day when he took me off the mountain. That means he'll be able to find me.

I don't quite know what to think about that, so I push it aside, keeping an eye out for any zintas who could be looking for me as I head toward the river.

This doesn't look like the part of the river that Dragix usually takes me to, the water rushing past much faster here. I walk along the water's edge and then stop, my mouth dropping open.

Is that a...ship?

It can't be. I've seen our ship, and this isn't it. I shake my head. Maybe our ship wasn't the first to crash-land on this planet.

Whatever it is, it's dangling half in and half out of the river. It's shaped kind of like an hourglass, and it looks utterly out of place in this otherwise peaceful and completely natural scene.

Movement draws my eyes, and then I'm hit with another bombshell. Two people are standing near the ship, and before I know it, I'm running.

"Alexis?"

"Charlie?"

I laugh. I remember this woman. And who wouldn't? She's gorgeous. So is the guy standing next to her, who examines me with cool eyes. He looks similar to the men who appeared in that clearing when the Voildi were leading us to the slaughter. Braxians.

Alexis slaps her hands over her ears, and I sigh as Dragix's enraged roar practically makes the ground shake.

Maybe he wasn't expecting me to get this far?

The Braxian next to Alexis shoves her behind him, a sword in his hand as he bares his teeth at us. Dragix lands in a crouch next to me, his complete attention on the two people across from us.

His voice snaps like a whip in my head. *"What are you doing? Who are these people?"*

"Calm down. Alexis is one of the women who were taken with me."

Dragix snarls at that, stepping forward slightly as he tucks his wings close to his body. He shows them his teeth and decides that this is a great time to let a flame escape his throat.

Even from here, I can see the color drain from Alexis's

face. I get it. I was so scared that I nearly peed my pants the first time I saw Dragix do that little trick.

I throw up my hands, hoping she'll see that I don't approve of Dragix's particular brand of crazy. But her eyes are on Dragix as he steps forward again.

I let out a growl of my own. *"What are you doing? You're scaring them!"*

"They're too close."

"You're being completely unreasonable. We're going to talk about this."

"Are you okay?" Alexis asks, and I take another step toward them. Dragix roars, making her slam her hands to her ears again, and I grit my teeth as I draw even with the dragon.

"You're being a complete bastard," I snap. "And it's embarrassing me."

He stares back at me silently, unrepentant, and I smack him on the snout with my fist. He narrows his eyes at me, and I turn back to Alexis and the silent Braxian at her side.

"I'm fine," I call to Alexis. "But—"

"Enough," Dragix seethes. His foot flies out, scooping me up, and I land on my butt. I probably look like a complete fool as Alexis's mouth drops open. I wave at her so she hopefully won't think that the enraged dragon is about to eat me.

Dragix is silent on the way back to his mountain. I don't even try to communicate with him, and he turns into a man as soon as he lands before stalking past me toward his lair.

"Oh, the silent treatment?" I throw up my hands, attempting to keep my gaze on the sloping muscles of his back and not his toned butt. "Real mature."

He glances back at me and bares his teeth, and then he's gone.

"Asshole," I mutter.

"Dragix allows more from you than I have ever seen him allow from anyone."

I whirl, finding Maez sitting in my shady spot.

"Well, since you're his lackey, you'd know."

She gazes at me steadily, and I sigh.

"That wasn't fair. I'm sorry."

She nods, getting to her feet.

"Why is he like this?" I ask.

"It is his story to tell."

"He doesn't share anything with me. And then he acts like a complete jerk when I finally get the chance to talk to one of the other women."

Maez hesitates, and then she steps closer, her purple skin gleaming in the sun. "Dragix has been alone for a very long time."

"How long?"

She shrugs, the movement elegant. "Centuries."

"Excuse me?"

"Dragons are very long-lived. After he lost his family, he was all alone. I don't know why he took you. He may not know himself. But consider what it must be like to be the only one of your kind. Always alone."

"He's not alone. He has you."

She shrugs again. "My people have always served the dragons. My mother served Dragix and her mother before her. My people swore to serve his people when they saved us from certain death."

"And then they were the ones who died."

Maez nods. "I am a reminder of his people. A reminder of a debt that was formed before he was born."

I turn away. "So what, just because he's lonely, he gets to treat me like a prisoner?"

Maez tuts. "My people were prisoners and slaves for

centuries before Dragix came to be, but their stories were passed on from generation to generation. You are not a prisoner."

I whirl on her. "I can't leave."

"And perhaps that is for your own protection." I open my mouth, and she waves a hand. "Dragix is not innocent. He takes what he wants because no one has ever told him that he can't. Or proved otherwise. I'm not going to try to change your mind about him. I just hope you have some room for understanding."

She turns and walks away, and I sit in the sun, staring up at the sky. Until I landed here, I'd never realized that there were so many shades of green. The fern green in the early morning, the bright emerald in the midday sun, and the golden-hued jade of the late afternoon combined with every shade in between.

What must it be like? To be so incredibly lonely that you steal someone you don't know and take them to your lair, just to have them around? And then keep them, even knowing they loathe being kept?

I know loneliness. I wouldn't wish it on anyone.

"Consider what it must be like to be the only one of your kind. Always alone."

I can't imagine centuries of being alone. Centuries without anyone who truly understands you. I wonder if that's why Dragix stayed in his dragon form. If that's why he forgot that he could shift back, that he could communicate. Maybe it was easier to stay the huge predator who could do whatever the hell he wanted than it was to turn back into the man who would always be alone.

I sigh and get to my feet. Then I head down the stairs until I'm finally hesitating at the entrance to the hot pools.

He's in there. Naked. *So* naked. And wet.

"I can smell you," he says mildly, and if I didn't know how pissed off he was, I'd think he was bored.

I go through the open door, finding him sprawled in the pool closest to me, gazing out at the lush forest.

No matter how much my greedy eyes want to explore the parts of him that lie beneath the water, I keep my eyes on his face.

"We need to talk."

He turns his head, and his eyes are pools of liquid gold. "I don't want to talk."

"Fine. You can listen."

I step closer, and then I'm in the air, falling as his hand snakes out and grabs my arm.

I shriek, but in an instant I'm underwater in the hot pool. With Dragix.

CHAPTER SEVEN

C harlie

I gasp as I clear the surface.

"What the hell?" I demand, my clothes sodden and heavy on my skin.

"I do not wish to talk, and you do. You do not wish to be in here with me. And I wish you to."

I grind my teeth. Dragon logic. Even worse than male logic.

"Okay," I snap. "Now that I'm in here with you, why don't you tell me why you lost your mind today?"

He snarls at me, and I simply stare at him, waiting. Then his eyes drop to my chest, where my shirt is clinging to my nipples, which have hardened beneath it.

The look he gives me is pure satisfied male.

I scowl at him and sit on one of the rocks in the pool, ensuring that the water covers me up to my shoulders.

His smile is slow, wicked, and so hot that I have to look away.

"I had just killed the Zintas that fired at us. They would have slaughtered you. If you were lucky. If you weren't, they would have taken you back across the Colossal Water and sold you to the highest bidder. And you would have wished you were dead."

I shiver. "The Colossal Water?"

He ignores that. "And then, when I came to find you, you were attempting to talk to my greatest enemy."

My eyes jump to his face. "Your greatest enemy?"

He shows me his teeth. "The Braxians killed my people."

"The Braxians?"

He nods, and I do the math.

"Are they as long-lived as dragons?"

"No."

It was their ancestors that killed his family. But he was around when it happened. Each time he sees a Braxian, he must remember.

I'm surprised he hasn't killed them all.

I must say that thought aloud because he tilts his head.

"I have thought about it. Their people landed on *our* planet using technology that they no longer have. Their swords are barbaric in comparison."

"How did they lose that technology?"

He gives a disinterested shrug of his shoulders and moves closer to me. I shiver at the look in his eyes.

"So why didn't you kill them?"

His jaw tightens. "Because they have females and younglings. My mother—" He breaks off and shakes his head. "My mother would be ashamed if I killed younglings."

I blink at that. The only thing stopping this giant

predator from burning this world to ash, from ripping everyone apart...is the thought of his mother.

My eyes sting. "I...I never had a mother," I say. "But I think yours would be proud of you. For not making the people here pay for what their ancestors did."

He's silent for a long moment, and I sigh. So when Dragix found me with Alexis, he'd just come from slaughtering the Zintas who would have killed us, or worse. Then he found me talking to one of the people who he still holds responsible for centuries of being alone.

"You acted like a jackass," I say. "But I get it."

His eyes widen slightly at that.

"I need you to promise me something," I continue, and he stays silent, his eyes on my face. "I need you to promise that you won't hurt the other human women. Or scare them."

His jaw tightens. "I told you I do not hurt females."

"I know, but if I see any of the other women again, I need you to try not to scare the hell out of them either."

He ponders this. "And the Braxians?"

"If you really need to swing your dick around, you can scare them. But no eating them."

"If I do this, you will be...pleased with me?"

I blow out a breath. "Yes. If you don't scare my friends, I will be pleased with you. Alexis is a nice woman, and she just wanted to talk to me. If you act like you could eat people at any moment, they're going to think that I'm not safe with you."

His expression darkens. "I do not care what they think."

"I do."

Liquid-gold eyes examine my face as he considers it.

"Fine," he says finally, and I feel my shoulders relax.

While I've got him in such an agreeable mood...

"I want to go see the other women."

"No."

"Dragix—"

He bares his teeth at me, and I frown at him. Obviously he's not feeling as agreeable as I thought.

"Why do you wish to leave me? Have I not kept you safe? Seared your food? Given you clothing?"

Over the past few weeks, I've learned a lot about this dragon. And one thing I've learned is that he's possessive as hell. What's his is *his*. He speaks of *his* lair. *His* territory. *His* Maez. And once, I heard him call me *his* Charlie.

I don't know how much of this trait is a dragon thing—after all, he's used to being the king around here—and how much is just...Dragix.

"You have," I say gently. "And if I haven't seemed grateful, I'm sorry. I really do appreciate everything you've done for me. Even if you did steal me in the first place."

He stares back at me, zero shame or remorse in his expression.

I almost laugh. "But humans can't be owned, Dragix. I'm not a pet. I have free will, and I want to be able to at least talk to some of the women I came here with."

"You are...lonely. I will spend more time with you."

I sigh. "That's not it, Dragix."

He moves closer. "You are disappointed with me."

"I don't know how to explain to you that you can't just take someone and keep them."

The lack of understanding in his eyes is all the confirmation I need. He believes he can. After all, he did.

I turn to go, and he pulls me back, setting me on my rock and then moving back to his spot.

"I cannot let you go to them, Charlie," he explains as if

I'm a small child, and I grind my teeth. "The Braxians are my enemies. What if they decide to keep you?"

"Do you truly think I'd let that happen? Besides, I thought they had a code of honor?"

"You may decide to stay."

"I won't."

He angles his head. "I will think on what you have said. I do not think you are a...pet."

I smile at that, but it feels like a sad smile. Then he smiles back.

"I find that I now understand why you spend so much time in these pools," he murmurs. "I am very...relaxed."

It's a blatant change of subject, but I have a feeling that the dragon has compromised as much as he's going to today.

I examine his face. From the look in his eyes, if I glanced beneath the water, I'd find that he's anything *but* relaxed.

"Yes," I say. "On that note, I'll leave you to your bath."

"You interrupted my bathing," he says. "You must give me something in exchange."

"Oh please," I say. "Get ahold of yourself."

He glances down beneath the water, and I slide off my rock, backing away. "I don't mean literally."

The puzzlement on his face is replaced by humor. "I would rather get ahold of you."

And then he pounces.

I squeal and dart to the side, but he's already anticipated my movement, and in the blink of an eye, he's holding his arms on either side of me, caging me in.

Ben stands in front of me, trapping me against the wall. "You should know better than to run from me," he snarls.

"Charlie. Charlie!" Dragix's voice is harsh, and I realize I'm shaking, suddenly freezing in the warm water.

"I'm okay."

"Why do you smell like terror?" He frowns. "Do you believe I'd hurt you?" The expression in his eyes is suddenly wounded, and I put my hands flat on his chest.

He's hot. So hot. And I'm so cold.

"No," I say, and I'm not lying. Somehow, over the past few weeks, I've learned to trust this dragon not to hurt me. It's ludicrous considering my past, but I trust the biggest predator of them all more than I trust human men.

"Then what is it?"

"My...ex. He used to trap me like this." I nod at his arms, and he instantly removes them.

He frowns, and I realize he doesn't get it. And why would he when he was raised by parents who taught him not to hurt women, even if you hold them personally responsible for your own family's deaths?

"He hurt me," I say, and his eyes blaze with fury. "And no, I don't want to talk about it. But that's why."

He stares at me, and I go to move away. Whatever weird moment we had going on here has disappeared. The lust in his eyes has been replaced with...pity.

It makes me grind my teeth.

"I don't think so," Dragix says as I go to scoot past him. "You still owe me."

I narrow my eyes at him, and he narrows his back.

"And what, exactly, do I owe you?"

"You interrupted my bath."

I roll my eyes. "For a man who hasn't used these pools in centuries, you're suddenly awfully possessive of your 'me time.'"

He ignores that. "And you're wearing clothes in the water."

"Because you pulled me in!" I can't help but laugh at the

sheer ludicrousness of his argument, and his eyes flare at the sound.

"I like your laugh," he announces. "Do that again."

His mouth is close to mine, and I can't help it. I do exactly what I've wanted to do since the second he shifted into a man.

I reach behind his head and pull his lips to mine.

He freezes, and I jolt away. "Oh God, did you not want to —I'm sorry."

He moves with me, but this time I don't feel caged. Now I just feel completely mortified.

"You touched your lips to mine."

"Yeah, look, I'm sorry. I obviously got the wrong idea." My cheeks are hot with mortification.

"Do it again."

I frown at him. "Kiss you...again?" He sure didn't seem to like the first time.

"Kiss..." He lingers over the word like it's a fine wine, and my mouth drops open.

His gaze instantly drops back to my lips.

"You've never...kissed anyone before?"

"My people do not do this." His eyes are gold flames as he brings them back to mine. "I do not know why."

I'm definitely getting in over my head here.

He moves closer still, and this time, he's the one who presses his lips to mine. He pauses, unsure of what comes next, and I sigh against his warm, firm lips. I brush my lips against his. Once. Twice. And then I lick his bottom lip, and he goes even more still against me.

"Is that okay?" I breathe against him, my body suddenly languid, overheated. We've done nothing except press our lips together, but the feel of him around me, the *hunger* in his eyes...

"More," he orders against my lips, and I can't help but let out a giddy laugh as I comply. I'm teaching a dragon how to kiss. How the hell did this happen?

I stroke my tongue against his lips again, and this time, he opens his mouth with a growl. He trembles against me as I brush his tongue with mine, and then he buries his hand in my hair and takes over, angling his mouth against mine as he thrusts his tongue into my mouth. I moan, and he growls back. I'm not sure which one of us is shaking more, but his other hand drops to my breast, finding my hard nipple and rolling it as I groan.

What am I doing?

I pull away, and Dragix lowers his head to follow me, but I put one hand on his chest.

"It's a little too hot in here," I say.

He inhales, and the temperature drops several degrees. I laugh. I'd forgotten about that little trick.

"That's not what I meant. I need to go and get dressed. I'm going to pick some berries. I'll see you later."

He frowns but doesn't stop me as I haul myself out of the water. I wring out my clothes and then step gratefully into the cool of the mountain.

What is wrong with me? Have I learned nothing from my experience with Ben? Or am I just a walking, talking victim who can't help but fall for overly possessive, dangerous men?

Men who believe I *belong* to them.

I made a promise to myself when I left Ben. A promise that I would never allow myself to end up in the same situation again.

I laugh, and my voice breaks. And here I am, cozying up to the dragon who stole me.

The worst part? He's *trying.* Unlike Ben, he truly doesn't

understand the idea of autonomy. He doesn't get that I wasn't put on this planet to entertain him. Because centuries of experience have taught him otherwise.

Ben was a sociopath. He chipped away at my confidence, my sense of *self,* for years. Until *I* forgot that I could be free. That I didn't have to live in fear. That I was worth something.

Dragix isn't a sociopath. At least, I don't think so. He's a different creature entirely. And he may try to see that I'm a person with free will, but he doesn't get it. He may never get it.

One kiss doesn't change that. Even if I *melted* for him.

I deserve better.

***

Dragix

After I finish bathing, I find myself restless. Usually, I would take to the skies, but I don't wish to leave Charlie, who is sitting in the shade on top of my mountain. Her eyes are on the trees below us, but they're blank, her mind elsewhere. Every part of her body is closed off, her shoulders hunched, arms crossed as she ignores me.

Fine.

I turn and walk back down into my lair.

I find myself in Ezra's room.

My sister would know what to say to me if she were here. She would laugh and explain the nuances that I don't understand. Of the two of us, she spent more time in her two-leg form and would often study the Braxians and other two-legs on this planet.

I miss her.

"I'm sorry," Maez says as she walks in, a bundle of clothes in her arms. "I didn't know you were in here."

I step back as she places the clothes on the bed and opens one of the large chests. She laughs at what she finds.

"Did you know Charlie was collecting these?"

I survey the chest, which has few clothes left, most of the space taken up by my...scales.

The sight makes something in my chest tighten. Charlie does not know that my scales are used as armor on this planet. Does not know that she could sell these and live like a queen on Agron. The first time I lost a scale when we were flying, she made me land so she could pick it up. She insisted it was *pretty*.

It does something to me. To see her collecting these small, discarded pieces of *me*.

"I did not."

Maez glances up at my face and then wisely chooses not to comment, opening another chest and placing the bundle in there instead. She keeps her eyes on the clothes and her voice low.

"Charlie has taught you more in days than you have learned in centuries. I'm happy to see you more like yourself. I have...missed the Dragix that I knew."

I examine her face. "I am sorry that I forgot I have this form. That I forgot who I was."

She glances up at me and then away, her dark hair falling over her purple skin. Seeing that movement, it reminds me of someone.

"Where is your mother?"

She stills. "You don't remember?"

"No." It is difficult for me to admit, and Maez pretends to ignore the gaps in my memory.

"When I was of age, she allowed me to take over from

her. Once I had completed the oath, she moved to Sebe with my father."

I remember now. The blood oath allows her people to be as long-lived as dragons. Maez's family have served my family for centuries, choosing to pass on the position when they want to grow old with those they love.

What would that be like? I push the thought away.

"Tell her...tell her thank you." Maez's mother served me during the years when I was most isolated, before I chose to spend all my time in my winged form. It is likely only due to the blood oath I have had with her people that I did not go insane during the long centuries I spent alone.

"I will."

CHAPTER EIGHT

C harlie

It's so hot today that I spend most of the afternoon napping in the cooler temperature of the lair.

Finally, when I start moving around, I find Dragix and beg him to take me to the river.

Hopefully, the water is just as cold as it was on the day that he showed me the hot pools.

He gazes at me, still in dragon form, and then nods his head. Neither of us has mentioned our kiss, although I often turn to find Dragix's hot eyes on me, as if he's ready to pick up right where we left off.

Surprisingly, Dragix doesn't love the heat either. I'm assuming that's why he spends most of his time on this mountain. While he can bask in the sun during the day, we're high enough up to still get a refreshing breeze, and the inside of the lair stays relatively cool even on the warmest days.

Over the past few days, he's spent most of his time in his dragon form. I don't know if it's because he tolerates the heat better in that form or if it's because it makes it easier for him to avoid me.

Whatever it is, he seems to become more...aloof as he spends more time in that form. More...predatory.

I don't like it.

He tilts his head, gesturing for me to come closer, and I step forward as he picks me up and places me on his back. He waits until I've hooked my legs around his neck, holding on to his horns. I've thought about riding further down, closer to the top of his back, but there's nothing to hold on to there.

"Does it hurt your neck when I sit here?" I ask suddenly, and Dragix snorts as he crouches, readying himself to shoot into the sky.

"Of course not. Your weight is minute. I would pay the same attention to an insect on my back."

"Wow, thanks for that."

He rumbles, and I realize he's making fun of me.

He stays in dragon form once we land, and I pad toward the river.

I raise my eyebrow at him. "You're not getting in?"

"No."

"Your loss."

I brought one of the long pieces of material that I use as towels with me, and I lay it over one of the rocks so it'll be warmed from the sun.

Then I glance at the river, at Dragix, and back again.

He angles his head, his eyes on my face.

"What is it?"

"I really want to strip off and jump in."

He displays his teeth, eyes dancing, and I realize he's giving me the dragon version of a shit-eating grin.

"Go right ahead."

I scowl at him. "You have to promise not to look."

A gust of warm wind hits me as he sighs. Then he's the one who glances between the river and my body.

"You plan to splash in that water unclothed and yet I cannot watch?"

"That's right."

He squints his eyes at me.

"This does not seem fair. I brought you to the cool water, and I don't even get rewarded with the sight of you enjoying it?"

I glower at him. "Life isn't fair, buddy."

I ignore what it does to my heart when he teases me. After the last few days of him ignoring me and me tiptoeing around while attempting to avoid thinking about that kiss, the amusement in his eyes is like a drug.

"Fine," he says with a huff. Then he curls up in the sun, the forest at his back, and angles his head away from me, facing the forest instead.

"Thank you."

It feels weird being naked outside. But not weird enough to stop me from pulling off my clothes and striding into the river.

The water is cold but not quite as bitterly cold as it was last time. It laps over my feet, and I sigh as I sink down into the water, shivering slightly as it hits my shoulders.

The sun beats down overhead, and I splash some of the cool water up my neck, sighing again at the relief from the hot weather.

"You are making the most interesting noises."

I glance over my shoulder, but Dragix is still facing away from me.

"You can get in here and feel why yourself as soon as I'm done."

He snorts.

I turn back to the river and shriek, crouching behind a huge rock. A woman is staring at me. A human woman from the ship. Ivy. I remember her because she helped me with my head wound. And she's walking hand in hand with a Braxian.

"You son of a bitch," I say. *"You couldn't tell me they were coming?"*

Dragix yawns, showing off his sharp teeth as he eyes our visitors. The Braxian is carefully keeping his eyes averted, and Dragix's gaze lingers on him.

"They are downwind. By the time I scented them, I could tell one of them was a female like you and would not harm you."

"Unless I die of embarrassment right here."

He lets out a rumble.

"Charlie?"

Ivy walks closer, and I huddle behind my rock like an idiot. I'm not completely shy, but I'd rather not walk around naked in front of three people. I glare at Dragix.

"You could hand me my towel, you know."

He sighs. *"When did I become your servant?"*

Dragix is entirely too amused, but he gets to his feet, picking up the towel from where I left it waiting on my rock. He throws it to me, and I wrap it around myself before walking back to the traitorous dragon.

Dragix once again flashes his teeth at Ivy and her Braxian.

I narrow my eyes at him. *"Scaring them is beneath you."*

I turn back to Ivy, who looks stunned. I can't entirely blame her.

"Um. Hi," she says, and I have to grin at that.

"Hi. Excuse the grumpy dragon. He hasn't had enough to eat today."

Dragix shifts behind me as the Braxian narrows his eyes at him.

They stare at each other, and then Dragix snorts.

*"I could eat **him**,"* he says.

I ignore that.

"He's not going to hurt you," I tell them. "We've come to an understanding."

Ivy looks doubtful, but she shrugs. "Uh, okay, then. We've been looking for you for a while now."

They have? While I imagined that these women were planning to leave without me, they've actually been actively searching for me?

I've never had many friends. Since I escaped Ben, I've never been in one place long enough to make friends. But these women, these...*strangers* have been trying to find me.

I feel like a giant asshole. Not only have I *not* convinced the dragon to let me find these women, but I haven't even tried to leave. Not for days.

"Yeah, I'm sorry," I say, my face heating. "It took a while before Dragix and I reached that understanding."

Ivy stares at Dragix, and I can see her wondering if I've just been talking to the giant dragon. Something tells me that he's not planning to open up that mental pathway to let her know that he really can talk.

"We've been in negotiations," I tell her. "I want to come hang out with you guys, but Dragix isn't the biggest fan of the Braxians."

Understatement of the century.

"That's why I'm here," she says. "We need your help."

"I'm listening."

Dragix is silent beside me, a huge blue-and-green guard dog, as Ivy paces on the riverbank across from us.

"Okay, so you know those purple bastards who bought us and loaded us onto their ship?"

"How could I forget?"

"Yeah. Well. We're pretty sure they're coming back."

My chest tightens as my mouth drops open, and just like that, I'm standing in front of hundreds of leering aliens while they negotiate how much I'm worth.

Then I'm forced to walk toward a ship, forced to watch as one of the other women falls to her knees and a purple alien kicks her in the ribs so hard that I can hear the crack.

"Breathe," Dragix orders, his voice sharp as a blade. *"Good. Again."*

Ivy pauses while I get ahold of myself.

Dragix moves closer to me. *"I do not like this. I do not like the scent of your terror. We will go now."*

"I need to listen to what they have to say, Dragix. I'm fine. Just give me a moment."

When I've pushed away the oncoming panic attack, I turn back to Ivy. She tilts her head sympathetically. They're not here. They can't hurt me. Can't steal us away. At least not right now.

I clear my throat. "What makes you think they're coming back?"

"The ship we were in. The one that crash-landed. Have you been inside?"

"No," I admit, feeling like a coward. Dragix narrows his eyes at me as if reading my mind.

"There's a light that flashes every so often. At least, when we landed here, it was every so often. Now it's flashing faster and faster each time we check it out. We're pretty sure that it's some kind of GPS signal. If I were an alien slaver and my people crashed a ship holding cargo I'd paid for, I'd come check it out. See if there were any survivors, anything to salvage, any products to recover."

I want to slam my hands over my ears. I want to tell her to go, to leave me alone, and I want to return to my mountain with Dragix.

His mountain. These women have been looking for me.

I shiver at the thought of the cruel aliens with the electric weapons that they used to herd us like cattle.

"You really think they're coming back?"

Ivy nods. "I think we should hope for the best but prepare for the worst."

I blow out a breath. I've lived that way for years. Why should this planet be any different?

Dragix moves even closer, nuzzling at me.

"You will be okay, little two-leg. I will keep you safe."

I smile at him, and then he glares at Ivy, obviously pissed that she upset me.

"It's not her fault, Dragix. She's just telling me the truth."

He snorts, and I stroke my hand down his nose.

Ivy clears her throat. "So what do you say?" she asks. "We're outgunned and likely to be outnumbered."

"I want to help," I say. I chew on my lip, and Dragix goes still beside me.

"You will not leave me to put yourself in danger," he says. *"I forbid it."*

I ignore that. "We need to discuss this," I say to Ivy, and she nods, her dark-red hair spilling over her shoulders. "But you can count on *my* help, even if *Dragix* doesn't quite feel up to the task."

Dragix tilts his head at my poor attempt at reverse psychology. *"Mind games mean nothing to me,"* he tells me, and I choose to ignore that too.

He's not pleased at my silence. *"We will go now,"* he says, his voice harsh. He reaches out and pulls me close, my clothes already clutched in the claws of his other foot. I roll my eyes, but it's evident that the dragon has used the last of his tolerance.

Not that he had a lot of it to begin with.

I don't argue, making sure the towel is wrapped around me fully as I sit down. Dragix extends his wings, and the color drains from Ivy's face.

"We'll talk about this," I tell her. "Tell everyone I'll come see them as soon as I can."

Dragix snarls and shoots into the sky.

***

Dragix

I don't speak as we fly back to my lair. And I can tell from Charlie's silence that she's disappointed in me. I swoop down and catch an udazin as it bolts across a clearing, biting down with a satisfying *crunch*. Charlie doesn't even wrinkle her nose when I glance down at her.

Instead, her mind is clearly elsewhere, her expression thoughtful.

Why would she want to join the other females when she would be in such danger? I scented her horror, her terror, as the other two-leg told her of these things. The reek of her fear was an affront to my nose.

Her voice sounds in my head. *"Humans can't be owned, Dragix. I'm not a pet."*

I snarl at that. For some reason, when Charlie is disappointed in me, it makes me want to growl. To growl and then beg for her forgiveness.

I narrow my eyes at that. Perhaps this is the problem. I have spent too much time with the little two-leg. She was not even a thought when I was born. And she will be dust in the ground before I am old.

The thought makes me roar, and Charlie glances up at me. She says nothing, and I don't attempt to explain myself.

I have spent too much time in my two-leg form. In that form, I become someone different. Someone who is more likely to give in to the whims of the female two-leg. Earlier today, when I lay on my rock, my mind clear, I remembered. I remembered why I must spend more time in this form.

My people have long known that to spend too much time as a two-leg is to invite mortality and eventually death. The old ones lived for thousands of years, seeing the topography of this planet change. When they were ready to leave this life and choose their place amongst the stars, they would take their two-leg form and let nature run its course.

I will never lose my life for a two-leg.

So why do you not allow her to leave?

I snarl again, and this time, Charlie rolls her eyes with a sigh. I show her my teeth, and she rolls her eyes again, examining her nails.

Maez's dark eyes float in front of my face. *"Charlie has taught you more in days than you have learned in centuries. I'm happy to see you more like yourself. I have...missed the Dragix that I knew."*

Perhaps...perhaps allowing her to go to her people is the best choice. The two-leg has accomplished what I did not imagine possible—she has drawn me from the apathy that haunted me for the last several centuries. She has allowed me to remember that I have two forms. That I can communicate. That I enjoy the feel of warm water on bare skin.

I am...grateful to her for that.

CHAPTER NINE

C harlie

We're both quiet over the next few days. Dragix is back in his dragon form, spending most of his time hunting and sleeping on his rock. I don't ask him to let me go to the other women again. I'm hoping that if he thinks about it enough, he'll realize on his own that it's the only solution.

And maybe a tiny part of me is putting off that conversation.

I'm...happy here. The traitorous voice in my head that pops up every so often urges me to stay with my dragon. It tells me that if he doesn't let me leave, I can't be held responsible for not helping the other women. For not risking being taken by the aliens who bought us. For not *leaving* this mountain.

And Dragix.

It's that voice that makes me look for Dragix when he's

not on the top of the mountain after his morning hunt. I'm a lot of things, but I've never been a coward.

Dragix is in the hot pools when I arrive. Instead of giving me the long, heated look I'm used to, he merely glances at me and then returns his attention to the forest.

"You still want to leave me."

"It's not that simple, Dragix."

His eyes jolt to mine at his name, and then he once again glances away.

This obviously isn't the time for our conversation. I turn to leave him alone, but his low, hoarse voice sounds behind me.

"Don't leave."

He's not just talking about right now, but I sigh and turn, sliding fully clothed into the tub. He smiles at me, but it's a sad smile.

"Dragix, you know you don't have to be alone. You're clinging to me because I was the first person you found after so long by yourself. But I'm sure you could easily find someone else who would want to live here with you."

My heart twists as I say it. Someone else who would fly on his back, nap with him in the sun...attempt to keep their hands off all the golden skin.

Except they wouldn't have to show any restraint. They could do whatever they wanted with my dragon. Kiss, touch, fuck...all of it.

I grind my teeth, jealousy stabbing through me.

No. I don't get to be jealous. Dragix deserves to be happy. I truly believe that now. And I forgive him for taking me. He wasn't in his right mind.

But someone will get this version of him. The Dragix with the slow smile, hot eyes, and playful words.

He tenses, and I remove my gaze from where it's drifted down to his chest.

"I don't want anyone else. I would rather be alone again."

"Dragix—"

"I don't wish to talk about this anymore."

I sigh, and he moves closer, his expression sad.

"Will you let me *kiss* you?" He lingers over the word, and I feel my cheeks heat. For the life of me, I can't think of a single reason to say no.

"Yes," I breathe, and in the blink of an eye, he's in front of me. I jolt. I forget sometimes how quickly he can move. How he can *pounce* when he sees something he wants.

And I'm something he wants.

He reaches out, and I blink as he takes me into his arms. I expected him to lean down and kiss me, but instead, he's reversed our positions so he's the one leaning against the rock and I'm now straddling him.

"You're tricky," I tell him, and he grins. His face suddenly looks so much younger, and I raise my hand, running it along his cheek. He closes his eyes and rubs his face against my hand like a cat.

It's like he's touch-starved. And I guess he is. Centuries alone. *Centuries.* With only Maez to talk to yet not remembering that he can. What must it have been like?

Hell. It must have been like hell.

I don't know how he survived it and came out the other side with his sanity intact.

"You...pity me."

Dragix's voice is a low growl, and he lifts me off him, his jaw tight.

"No, Dragix. I admire you. I think it must take a special

kind of man to spend so much time as a predator, forget most of what makes you who you are, and still choose not to destroy the people who you hold responsible for your loneliness."

"My mother—"

"She sounds like an amazing woman. But it was still *you* who had to make the choice. Every day, you chose not to seek revenge. She'd be so proud of you. *I'm* proud of you."

His smile is a beautiful thing. His hands are still on my butt, and I lean close, almost unable to help myself as I nip his bottom lip.

He goes so still that he barely breathes. So I do it again, this time adding a stroke of my tongue. He growls, and one of his hands slides up from my butt as he buries it in my hair and takes my mouth.

How did he get so good at kissing? If I didn't know, without a doubt, that he hasn't been practicing on other women, I'd have my suspicions. But Dragix is obviously just a fast learner, and I groan against his mouth as he strokes my tongue with his, angling my head so he can get deeper, then teasing me as he pulls away.

This time, I'm the one to grab the back of his head and pull him back to me.

He lets out a laugh that's wrapped in pure male satisfaction.

I grind down on him, feeling him hard and long and thick against me. My thin pants are no protection from the heat of him.

I don't want them to be.

Now he's the one to groan as I twist my hips and writhe against him, pleasure gliding up my body. He moves his other hand under my shirt, up my abdomen, to where my nipple is hard and aching.

"I have gaps where my memories should be," he growls

against my lips. "But all my instincts tell me that you are the most beautiful thing I've ever seen."

My throat tightens, and I swallow around the lump that forms at his words. I haven't even left this man yet, and I already miss him so deeply that it feels like I have my own gaps. Dragix-sized gaps.

His hands are sure and unhesitant as he moves one of them back to my butt, using it to help me grind on him while his other hand plays with my nipple. He pinches and rolls, and I lean forward for another slow, deep kiss.

"Ahem," a female voice sounds.

"You have *got* to be kidding," I murmur against his mouth, and Dragix slowly pulls his head away, his eyes liquid gold as he keeps them on my face.

He leans toward me again, and I slap one hand over his mouth. He frowns at me and then turns his attention to Maez, his expression dark.

To her credit, she doesn't tremble at the look in those eyes.

"The Zintas," she says. "They're in your territory. Hundreds of them."

I shiver at the rage on Dragix's face as he gently lifts me off him and gets to his feet. His cock is hard and thick, and I have a sudden urge to cover it up in front of Maez.

She's not looking though, her eyes almost wild as she keeps them on his face.

"Where are they?" he asks.

"The southeast border. The came across the Colossal Water in large numbers."

"What do they want?" I ask.

Maez flicks her gaze to me. "His scales. His blood. They don't realize that it's not dragon blood that heals but saliva."

I stand, the lust that was pouring through my body

instantly replaced with outrage. "Why do they want his scales?"

"Armor," Dragix says as he climbs out of the hot pool. "They sell it for people to use as armor."

"I'm coming with you."

He shakes his head, and I get out of the pool, water running off my clothes in a flood.

"You would split his attention," Maez says softly as Dragix stalks back into the cool mountain and we trail after him. "He would be consumed with keeping you safe."

She's right. I know she's right. I've seen how protective Dragix is of me. But I wish there was something I could do.

"I want to help."

Dragix is stalking up the stairs, and I attempt to keep my eyes off his tight, toned butt.

Now is not the time, Charlie.

Maez glances at me, and from the way her mouth twitches, she obviously knows what I'm thinking. But then her face sobers.

"If you want to help, be here when Dragix returns. He will not be...himself after killing so many of his enemies. But I believe you will be able to calm him."

She doesn't mention the scene she just walked in on, and I nod.

Dragix turns to us as we get to the top of the mountain, and I shiver at the expression on his face. Wrath. Pure, unrelenting wrath. I almost feel sorry for the Zintas.

But they were the ones shooting at us that day. The ones that managed to hit his wing with an arrow. He pulled it out, healing quickly, but what if they all fire on him? I get a vision of him roaring as he falls to the ground, pinned by hundreds of arrows, and my heart almost stops.

"Don't be afraid," he tells me, his nostrils flaring. "I will protect you."

"It's you I'm worried about."

He snorts at that, shifting instantly to his dragon form. I stride forward and place one hand on his snout, looking into those glorious eyes. "Be careful. Please."

He nods and then gestures for me to back away. He glances at Maez.

"I'll keep her safe," she vows, and I grind my teeth. I hate, *hate,* that I'm the weakling human who would be nothing but a liability right now.

Dragix shoots into the sky so fast that he's like a bolt of lightning. Here one moment and in the sky the next.

***

Charlie

I sit on top of the mountain while I wait for Dragix to get back.

It's been years since I trusted a man to touch me like that. Years since I lost myself in the feel of strong male arms around me.

Now that he's gone, my head is clearing. What I'm doing...it's dangerous. I don't believe that Dragix would ever hurt me. Deep down in my soul, I know he would never raise a hand to me. But I've been wrong before. And Dragix is different from Ben. When I met Ben, I was young, innocent, naive. Now I'm older, jaded, and well aware of the lies that men tell to get you to drop your guard.

Dragix doesn't lie. He's honest to a fault. He doesn't think to deceive me because he doesn't have to. He has the strength and power to do whatever he wants to me, yet he makes me feel *safe*.

And that's the problem. Am I falling into old habits?

When the Arcav invaded, a tiny part of me hoped that I'd be an Arcav mate. That someone would save me from the torment. From the endless violation of restraining orders and constant, gut-twisting fear. When I tested negative, I sobbed in the bathroom, wishing I had a way out of my life. That I could just leave Earth behind.

I was considering applying to travel to Arcavia for work. To settle on the planet.

And then I watched as Harlow, the Arcav king's mate, ran. Just like I did. How she fought back and was taken to Arcavia anyway.

I destroyed my application form—which I'd had to purchase on the black market. It was only when I saw how in love they were, how the Arcav king bent, how he changed the laws, how he *listened* and gave human women back their rights that I regretted my decision.

And then Ben found me again, and the cops in Austin told me to file a different type of restraining order.

They don't tell you that those restraining orders are going to really piss off your abuser—and that if you're going to get one, you also need a backup plan so you can run like hell. They don't tell you how many women end up dead anyway, the restraining orders they counted on to protect them tucked away in their purses or shoved into drawers.

They don't tell you that if he ever strangles you—if he ever gets enraged enough that he's trying to choke the very air from your lungs and you're lucky enough to survive—the chances that he'll kill you increase significantly.

I rub my throat, feeling his hands, huge and strong, around me, cutting off my air. I get to my feet, forcing myself to take deep breaths. For the first time, I have a chance to process, a chance to look back on the last few years.

I was able run because I had no ties. My parents were dead, and I had no kids. So I was able to move every time I felt someone watching. Every time I realized he'd hired another private investigator to find me.

It's sheer luck that I'm alive.

What if I...didn't go back?

What am I returning to anyway? A life of living in my car, shaking awake through nightmares, and constantly looking over my shoulder.

I push the thought away. And what would I do on this planet? Dragix will get bored of me eventually. I'm the shiny new thing he has to play with, the pet that drew his attention. We both know that I'll be dead in decades compared to his centuries.

Maybe...maybe if I can talk to the other women, I can see what they're doing here. They must have some way to support themselves. I could work, cook, clean, whatever I need to do.

Dragix's scales flash through my mind. *Armor,* Dragix said. If I got desperate, I could sell them.

The thought is abhorrent, and I instantly reject it. If I leave Dragix, there's no way I can give up the small pieces of him I'll have left.

Don't be an idiot, Charlie. You'll do whatever it takes to survive. Like you always do.

Dragix

I shudder with pain as I fly toward my mountain. A trap. The Zintas marching on my territory had been a trap, a way to distract me while the creatures hiding in the trees attacked. They were covered in mud to dull their scents, and it took me too long to realize that their arrows were coming from every direction.

A large portion of my territory is now little more than ash.

As are the Zintas.

They were well armed, however. My wings are torn, injuries that will take at least a day to mend even with my unique healing abilities.

Dizziness overtakes me, and my blood drops through the air like rain. I fight against the urge to close my eyes. If I fall, I will be completely vulnerable to any creatures who come across my unconscious body.

Charlie is waiting on my mountain, pacing. As I get closer, she turns, hands on her hips, shock clear on her face as I approach.

My landing is sloppy, my wings no longer able to support my weight.

"Move!" I order, terror shooting through me at the thought of landing on top of her.

She leaps out of the way, and I crash with a thump that makes my mountain shake.

"Oh God, oh God, Dragix, are you okay? Jesus, there's so much blood."

"I am...fine."

My voice sounds weak, even to me, and I snarl. Never should a male of my species show weakness. But those are

Charlie's cool hands on my snout, Charlie's deep-blue eyes on mine.

"Shift back," she orders me shakily. She glances over her shoulder as Maez arrives, out of breath. She runs to my side, her face shocked.

Charlie leans closer, her eyes wild. "Shift before you pass out, Dragix. We can't help you properly in this form."

I reach for the shift. And it's agonizing. Pain rips through my body as I shift around the arrows stuck into me. Some of them fall, torn from my skin, yet still more remain.

"What do we do?" Charlie's voice is panicked.

"We must remove the arrows," Maez replies. "Once they are no longer in his body, he will be able to quickly heal the wounds."

Maez leans over me, her expression grim. "You will need to prepare yourself."

Charlie is shaking next to me. "How can I help?"

I take her hand, pulling her close. Her worried gaze meets mine. "Maez will do it."

"Stay close to him," Maez tells her. "Make sure he can breathe in your scent as I work."

I shift my attention to Maez and see the awareness in her eyes. She knows. Knows that my dragon has almost mated with the two-leg. That the most basic primitive part of me will be reassured by Charlie's scent and that it will prevent me from shifting and ripping Maez apart when she causes me even more pain.

"Look at me," Charlie murmurs, moving even closer. Her face is pale, and she raises my hand to her face, placing a gentle kiss on my palm. "I'll distract you."

Maez pushes one of the arrows through my thigh, and I can feel my blood draining from my body.

I snarl.

"Shh," Charlie soothes. And it's the steady, deep blue of her eyes that keeps me grounded. That allows me to tolerate the pain.

Tears are dripping down her face and onto mine by the time Maez works on the arrow that has lodged itself in my gut.

"You're lucky this wasn't a little to the left," she murmurs. "You may not have made it back here."

Charlie lets out a sob, and I ignore the pain as I soothe her. "I would have made it back to you," I reassure her, and she gives me a shaky smile.

The next minutes are agonizing. Finally, finally, Maez pulls away. "I'm finished," she says. "Can you shift?"

"No." It is difficult to admit that I'm too drained to reach for my other form. I would heal slightly faster in my winged form, would be more able to protect the females under my care.

"Shh," Charlie says as I attempt to move. "It's okay, Dragix. If you can't shift now, you can do it later."

I nod, fighting the rage. For the first time in centuries, I am...weakened.

And I know why.

Too much time in two-leg form has consequences. Slower healing being one of them. Yet I will never regret spending time with Charlie. Never regret touching her skin, kissing her lips.

"I'll be right back, okay?" Charlie murmurs, glancing at Maez.

Maez nods. "I'll stay with him."

We sit in silence as I gaze up at the sky.

"I have never seen you so wounded before," Maez says.

"I am weaker," I reply and meet her gaze. She nods, obviously understanding what is happening to me.

"Will you tell Charlie?"

I frown. "No. And you won't either. She will feel responsible for this."

Maez frowns at me and opens her mouth—likely to argue—but we both turn our heads as we hear Charlie panting and cursing.

She appears, walking backward and dragging a mattress with her.

Maez gets up and helps her maneuver the mattress close to me.

"I wanted to bring a larger one up here, but there was no way I could get it up the stairs," Charlie says apologetically, still slightly breathless. "I figured this might be more comfortable."

I smile at her. The sun will be going down soon. "Will you stay with me?"

She nods as Maez helps her push the mattress next to me. "Do you need help?"

I give her a look, and she throws up her hands with a grin. "Fine. God forbid I damage your fragile male ego."

It takes all my remaining energy to roll onto the mattress, which is stuffed full of feathers. I'm panting and covered in a fine sweat by the time I'm lying on top of it. Part of me is enraged at this new weakness.

The other part of me wonders if I can convince Charlie to lie with me.

I glance at her. "Will you lie on this mattress with me?"

She nibbles on her lip. "Is that what you want?"

"Of course."

She finally smiles and sits on the edge of the mattress. I reach out, and she yelps as I pull her down until my arm is wrapped around her and she is lying on my chest.

It aches, but the feel of Charlie in my arms is worth it.

Maez smiles at us. "I will leave you alone. Let me know if you need anything."

We watch the sun go down, and I slowly feel some of my strength return to me. Charlie is draped over me, obviously tired, but she brushes her hand over my chest, dancing over a large bruise.

"I'm still confused as to how it could be worth it. How the loss of so many of their men could be worth some armor and potentially some greater healing abilities," she says.

I shrug and instantly regret the movement. "There will be someone powerful at the top. Someone who wants to use my scales as a symbol. He will use them to make armor, which he will wear in front of his people, and he will tell them that he can now heal anything, that he is immortal."

"But he won't be. He'll just have your blood. And it won't do anything...right?"

"His people won't know that."

"It's insane. The loss of so much life for a symbol."

"Leaders will always need symbols for their followers— the people too stupid or too cowardly to choose their own paths. People looking for an excuse to hurt, to destroy, to kill. It would never occur to those men to question their orders. To choose to be more than mindless soldiers. To not attack the biggest threat to their safety."

Charlie nods against me, and her voice is small when she lifts her head. "Are they still here? In your territory?"

"I killed them all," I tell her.

She leans over and kisses the tip of my nose. "Of course you did," she says, and her tone is satisfied.

I smile at her. "Wicked female."

She kisses my lips. "They came into your territory. Tried to *kill* you. Scared the life out of me. All because they want your scales, your blood. I'm not sorry that they're dead. I'm only sorry that they didn't know better than to attack in the first place."

"I am not unaware like my people were."

Charlie studies my face, and I wonder what she sees. "What do you mean?"

"We lived on this planet for thousands of years before the Braxians arrived. When they landed in their metal ships, we did not think anything of it. They waited until the longest day of the year—when we are all together, the night when so many younglings first take to the sky, the elders ready to catch them."

"Oh God."

I nod. "I was one of those younglings. But I had been practicing in secret. When they began shooting the younglings out of the sky, the elders rose, went hunting." My throat hurts at the memory, and I shift restlessly. The physical pain is slightly better.

"They were killed too," Charlie says.

I nod. "My father rounded up some of the younglings who had not yet been killed and told us to hide. He told me to protect them. The Braxians had a ship. A ship with weapons that they turned on my people." My voice is hoarse.

"But you survived."

"Yes. I was injured, but I survived. I had landed in the forest, fallen into a pile of leaves. I was too wounded to move, and it was little more than luck that kept me alive when they hunted everyone else over the next few days."

Charlie's eyes are wet. "Why? Why did they do it?"

"They are descended from dragons—not my people but dragons from their planet. Braxians can no longer shift. Perhaps they were hunted on their planet. Perhaps they decided that they were unwilling to be prey again—unwilling to risk living so close to my people."

"There's no excuse," Charlie snaps. "None."

I take one of the spirals of Charlie's hair and pull on it, watching in fascination as it springs back into place. *Curls*, I remember.

"No," I say. "There isn't. Maez's family found me and helped me heal. When I was large enough, I hunted the Braxians for sport, killing large numbers of them. They were almost extinct like my people when more of them arrived."

"You didn't kill them."

"No. By then, the worst of the rage had passed, and I could almost hear my mother's voice in my head, telling me that the new arrivals shouldn't pay for what had been done to my people. But I created my territory and made it clear that any Braxian who dared come close would die screaming."

"I'm so sorry, Dragix."

"So am I. You should sleep, little two-leg," I say simply to see her smile at the nickname.

"What about you?"

"I will sleep too."

But I spend hours staring at the stars, wondering which of the glimmering lights are my parents.

CHAPTER TEN

C harlie

I wake to gentle kisses on my face, down my neck, on the arch of my ear. I open my eyes to see Dragix's face above me, and then his mouth is hard, dominating.

I moan as his tongue strokes mine.

"Dragix," I mumble, pulling back slightly. "Your wounds."

"Healed," he says. "Sore but healed. Please, little two-leg. Be with me."

How could I do anything else? Yesterday, when I watched him fall, realized how close I'd come to never seeing him again...it almost killed me.

"Yes," I breathe, and his eyes widen as if he can't believe his luck.

Dragix is naked, as usual, but he helps me peel off my clothes. I blow out a shaky breath, suddenly nervous, and he pauses above me.

"You are scared." He goes to move back, and I reach out, pulling him close.

"No, no, not like that. It's just been a long time. And as I couldn't help but notice, you're not exactly small."

His grin is wicked, his hands gentle as they stroke over me, his touch almost reverent.

"We will go slow," he says, and then he leans down, once again taking my mouth with his.

His hands explore my body as his tongue explores my mouth. I'm tense, almost shaking against him, desperate for more when he pulls away. Sending me another smile, he begins kissing his way down my body.

My mouth goes dry at the sight of his golden head moving down as his lips caress me, slowly driving me crazy.

"You steal my control," he murmurs, gazing up at me, his eyes burning.

"Right back atcha," I manage to reply, but the words turn into a moan as he takes one of my nipples in his mouth.

I wind my fingers into his hair, holding him to me as I gasp. He runs the edges of his teeth lightly against my peaked nipple, and I almost climax right there.

He gives me a wicked, wicked smile, as if he just read my mind. I stare him in the eye and scoot down slightly beneath him until I can reach the long, hard heat of him.

I wrap my hand around him, raising my eyebrows as I find that my fingers don't quite meet.

"This is a little intimidating," I say, and he closes his eyes, shuddering above me.

"I would never hurt you," he manages to get out, and I let out a hum of agreement as I lean up and press my own kisses to his chest.

He grasps my hair, using it to angle my head and taking my mouth once more. His tongue strokes against mine as if he's starving for the taste of me, as if he'll never get enough.

I feel the same.

Then he leans down and takes my hand from his cock, pressing a kiss to my palm.

"Allow me to play first," he says, and I open my mouth to protest, but in the blink of an eye, he's already between my legs, gently pulling off the loose pants I wore to bed.

I blush as he studies me, and then I squirm as he gazes up at me. He looks at me like I'm candy and he has the world's biggest sweet tooth.

His hand slides over me, and my cheeks feel even hotter at the sound of my wetness. He groans, and his expression is possessive as he slides his finger inside me. He kisses my inner thighs, using his tongue to make me shiver. I'm so sensitive there, and my shiver seems to delight him as he does it again and again.

"Dragix…"

His finger begins to move, and he adds another, filling me up. He shifts his mouth to my clit and blows on it gently, watching as I writhe.

"Dragix…" He grins up at me, and I can't help but let out a breathy laugh. "You look far too pleased with yourself."

He withdraws his fingers, and then he's pressing himself to me, rubbing against me. I spread my legs even further, and he gently eases inside me. He goes slow, careful not to hurt me, and I'm so desperate for him that I'm the one lifting my hips, encouraging him to move faster.

"Gently, Charlie," he murmurs. He leans down and nibbles against my lips, and then with one smooth thrust, he's filling me up. He leans back and stares at me, and I'll remember the look on his face for the rest of my life.

Tenderness, elation, and desperate need. He kisses me

again, and then he moves, easing in and out as my body becomes used to him, so large, inside me.

"I don't need you to be careful anymore," I murmur, twisting my hips. He groans as I tighten around him, and then he plunges into me as we both gasp.

I can hear someone moaning, and I realize it's me. I'm close, so close, and I pull him down, pressing myself against him as he grinds into me with each thrust, hitting my clit.

My body trembles, spasming around him, and I cry out as he thrusts again and again until it seems like the pleasure will never end. I come once more, my orgasm ripping through my body as I gasp, and this time he comes with me, burying his face in my neck with a growl.

We're quiet for a long time as I stroke my hand down his back. I don't know about him, but I feel vaguely shell-shocked. I didn't know sex could be like that. Didn't know I could be so undone by pleasure that I could barely remember my own name.

Dragix lifts his head and grins at me, as if we're two children who have gotten away with something we shouldn't have. I laugh, and he slowly moves off me, rolling over onto his back and taking me with him.

"Are you sure you feel okay?" I murmur.

"I could not feel better. Tell me about your life," he says softly, his breath warm against my neck.

"There's not much to tell," I hedge, and he pulls me up his body so he can look into my eyes.

"I want to know everything about you, little two-leg."

I laugh. "You know, that's a ridiculous nickname."

He smiles, tracing my mouth with his finger. "Tell me."

"Well, to be honest, I didn't have much of a life," I admit. "I was living in my car in Houston when I was taken. I wonder if that was why it was easy for the Grivath to take me. I haven't talked to the other women about where they were taken from."

"What is a car?"

I explain—as best I can—how a car works.

Dragix frowns. "Why did you not have a home, like this one?" He gazes at the rock walls surrounding us, and I can't help but laugh.

"No one has a home like this one, buddy," I say with a laugh. "I was...running. From my ex."

"Your lover," he says, his face hardening, and I nod. "Why were you running?"

I take a deep breath. "It's hard to talk about. Women on Earth...one in three of us are abused by our partners. It's a sick club that I belonged to. I think it's getting better, now that the Arcav are there. At least for those that are mates."

"Your lover...hurt you?"

I nod, and Dragix's face flushes with fury. And then I stare as his body slowly begins to turn shades of blue and green. He trembles against me.

"Dragix?"

"I am sorry," he says. He grits his teeth, fighting the shift, and his skin reverts back to smooth gold silk.

"I wish I could travel to your planet," Dragix murmurs. "Why is he not dead?"

"That's not really how it works," I say. Dragix blinks in incomprehension, and despite the topic, I have to hold back my smile.

"Why did no other males help you?"

I almost laugh at the sheer misogynism in that question, but on a planet as barbaric as this one, the question is valid.

I try to explain. "It's not like he just hit me out of nowhere. We met at a club in New York originally. He was in the VIP section, and I was celebrating my friend's engagement. He was loving at first. Charming. I'd never dated anyone like him."

Dragix snarls at that, and I stroke my hand up his back. My possessive dragon. Somehow, his jealousy doesn't scare me the way it should. And maybe that's a red flag in itself.

"It started with backhanded compliments, veiled insults. I never went to college—my parents died in a car accident when I was a teenager, and they had no life insurance." I wave a hand. "Never mind. Basically, I had no support. I was seventeen and all alone when they died. My grades plummeted, and I had no hope of scholarships. So the moment I turned eighteen, I took a job waiting tables.

"Ben was a high-priced defense attorney. When we first got together and I did something to piss him off, that's what he would throw in my face. My lack of education. My minimum-wage job. He'd make jokes about it, sometimes in front of his friends."

I clench my fists at the reminder of the humiliation of it all.

"I was so young. So alone. Looking back on it now, I was the perfect target. When he said I should quit my job, that it wasn't bringing in any money anyway, that it embarrassed him, I did it. He said he wanted to spoil me, to take care of me." Dragix's eyes are hot on my face, and I shake my head. "It doesn't matter now."

"No," he says, his voice hoarse with rage. "Finish it."

I swallow. Maybe it's best to get it out. So I can finally take the first step toward forgiving myself.

"The first time he hit me, it was because I wouldn't let him read my texts. He was being stupid, and I told him so. He slapped me across the face, and I stood there like an idiot, in shock." Dragix inhales, and the air around us goes cold. My eyes widen, and he simply gestures for me to continue.

I sigh. "He apologized profusely, bought me flowers, and treated me like a princess for the next three months. I thought it was a one-off. He was stressed with work.

"Long story short, by the time I finally left, I had no friends to call. I'd basically disappeared. They thought I'd been too wrapped up in my new relationship to care about them anymore, and I had nowhere to go. They would've helped me if I'd told them. If I'd let them know what Ben had done to me. But I was too ashamed. I moved out, and he found me. Then I moved again, and he found me again. The threats, the pleading, the constant fear—it got to be too much. I thought I loved him. So I went back."

A tear rolls down my face, and Dragix kisses it away. "You were alone and scared."

I nod. "And weak."

He catches my chin in his hand. "No."

I shrug, still disappointed in myself. "A few weeks later, I did something to annoy him. I don't remember what it was. All I remember is that he wrapped his hands around my throat."

Dragix pulls me close, his huge body shaking as he kisses every inch of my face. I sigh, catching his lips with mine.

His lips are warm, gentle. He kisses me like I'm precious.

"You survived."

"Yeah. A stroke of luck. He'd forgotten that one of his friends was about to arrive. He told me to go into the bedroom and shut the door. I did, and while I was there, I shoved whatever I could find into my backpack. And the moment he took his friend into the living room, I bolted down the hall and straight to the police."

And then I spent three years on the run.

Dragix's brow creases and then he draws away from me. "And then you landed here, and I took you and stopped you from leaving. Stealing your freedom away. No wonder you hated me. No wonder you want to leave."

I shake my head. "Yes, when you first took me, I thought you were just like Ben. But you're not, Dragix. You'd never hurt me. If you didn't do it when you were more beast than man, you won't do it now. I know that deep in my bones."

"I will take you to the other two-legs tomorrow," he says, and my mouth drops open.

"What?"

"If I do not give you your freedom, I am no better than the male who tormented you for so long."

My eyes sting. The dragon learned about autonomy. About freedom. For me.

I gaze down at him. I don't want to go, and that's why I need to. This is the smart choice. The only choice.

Dragix

I mate with my little two-leg over and over again, throughout the day and night. I do not yet trust my wings to hold us, so I will have one more night with Charlie before I give her her freedom.

Guilt plagues me at the thought of her terror when I took her. Not just because I was a creature that she had never seen before but because she had already been abused.

I am...ashamed.

"You're thinking about it again," Charlie says softly, and I glance down at her. When the day began to heat, we moved down to what was once my parents' room. The room is large enough for me to lie in dragon form, which would help me heal.

But I don't want to miss a moment of this. Of lying with Charlie, *my* Charlie.

She sighs at my silence. "I forgive you, Dragix. You never hurt me, not even that night when I tried to escape."

"I would *never* harm you."

"I know."

The sun is rising, the room turning a light gray. If I do not make myself take her soon, I will not be able to.

"We should go."

Charlie sits up, her dark hair tousled around her beautiful face. "Are you sure? Can you fly?"

I nod. "We will go now." Before I change my mind.

She suddenly looks so sad that I have to turn away.

"I will meet you upstairs," I say.

"Okay." Her voice is small. "If that's what you want. I'll go say bye to Maez."

I nod and stalk out. Maez will not understand my choice. Suddenly, I regret ever seeing that ship fall from the sky. Regret ever being curious enough to fly toward it, to investigate the scent that drew me. If I had resisted the urge, I would have stayed in my winged form, never knowing any different. Never knowing this...loss.

But then you would not know Charlie.

She is wearing billowy dark-gray pants and a shirt the color of her eyes when she steps out onto the top of my mountain. She's clutching a bundle in her arms, and I can smell my scent. My scales. She looks fragile, and sad, and so beautiful that I have to turn away as I shift into my winged form.

It hurts, but I embrace the pain. I would rather feel this pain than the pain of losing Charlie.

"Dragix..."

"We will go now."

Her expression is sad when I finally look at her, and I have to glance away as a tear drips down her cheek.

"Okay," she says softly. "You're right."

I help her onto my back and stretch my wings, ignoring the ache that lingers from the healing. I eat three udazin as we fly and immediately feel less drained.

And I take my little two-leg to her new home.

CHAPTER ELEVEN

C harlie

Thanks to the tears streaming from my eyes, I can't even enjoy my last flight with my dragon. Dragix, thankfully, gives me privacy while I cry, but I know he can likely smell the salt from my tears.

He eats a few animals along the way, and it seems to help him fly faster. I hope he's completely healed, but I've got a feeling that he's still not yet at his best.

I wipe my face as he moves lower, no longer using his wings but soaring on an air current.

This is the smart choice. The right choice.

So why does it feel like shit?

Dragix lands, and I realize I've paid no attention to where we are. We're in a small clearing close to a forest, and he transforms as I watch.

"The other two-legs are through there," he says, pointing.

I'm not ready to leave him. "Will you...come with me?"

He studies me, and I wonder if he's internally cursing me for making this even harder. But he nods, reaching for my hand.

"Wait. Maez gave me these for you." I reach into my sack of clothes and beneath the precious scales I've collected. Finally, I find what I'm looking for, and I hand Dragix the pants. I knew that small line would appear between his eyes. That his lower lip would jut out just the tiniest bit. Not a pout but a clear sign of his displeasure.

"Come on, Dragix," I wheedle, holding up the pants. "Don't you want to see where I'll be staying? To meet the other women?"

He hesitates, staring at the pants, and then meets my eyes. "This is what you want?"

"You don't have to if you don't want to." I sigh. "Honestly, I'm not ready to say goodbye to you yet."

That makes his gold eyes lighten slightly, and he looks at me for a long moment. "If this is what you want, I will come with you."

"I realize I'm asking you to get close to your enemies. If you don't want to do it..."

He angles his head as he gazes at me. "I would like to see these other two-legs. To know that you will be safe with them."

It makes my heart hurt, but I nod, and he takes the pants, pulling them on. It feels incredibly weird to see him clothed—like watching a tiger put on a pair of shoes.

I thought it would make him look more civilized, but the way he tilts his head, looking down at his pants in distaste, makes it obvious that he's not exactly a fan of clothes.

"Thank you," I say.

He nods, and I take his hand as we walk in the direction he pointed.

It's not long before a Braxian approaches, his eyes widening as he sees me.

"A human female," he manages to get out, stuttering a little. "You are the one who has been missing."

I nod. "I'd like to talk to the other women, please."

He stares at Dragix, and I glance at him, almost laughing. The dragon has obviously decided to attempt to look unthreatening. His hands are by his sides, and he's ducking his head, avoiding the Braxian's eyes.

The Braxian hesitates and then finally turns. That's when Dragix raises his eyes, and I catch the look in them.

Pure, unwavering fury.

I must make some sound because he shifts his gaze to me, and his eyes soften slightly.

"You know what? We don't need to do this," I say. "This was a dumb idea, I'm sorry."

He shakes his head. "I find that I need to see that you will be safe here," he says.

My chest tightens. How could I have ever thought that Dragix would harm me? Not only is he giving me my freedom, but he's getting close to his enemies just to make sure I'll be safe.

I nod and squeeze his hand. And then we're following the Braxian into a huge, sprawling camp. There are tents everywhere, and while Dragix explained that the Braxians are usually nomadic, nothing about this camp looks temporary.

"Charlie?"

I turn, and my mouth drops open at the woman who is trotting toward me. Her bump is small, but she's still visibly pregnant, and she beams at me as a huge Braxian follows her, his gaze scanning me and then landing on Dragix, where it lingers.

"Ellie, right?"

She nods, and it's hard to reconcile this happy woman with the one who had a broken arm and looked like she was about to pass out when we were following the Voildi.

"We've been looking for you for weeks."

"Wow, it doesn't feel like it's been that long."

"Nevada," Ellie calls over my shoulder, and I turn as I see another woman standing near a pen of weird scaled creatures that would be similar to horses if they weren't bright green and horned.

Nevada turns, and her eyes widen as she spots me.

"Well hell," she calls as she strides toward us, and I feel a moment of envy for her long legs, showcased in tight leather pants. "Here we are coming up with plan after plan to find you, and you end up strolling right in the front door."

I remember this woman. She was the one who told the Voildi we were going to stop so I could rest. She grins at me and then gestures to some of the other women.

It's a little overwhelming, having the same conversation over and over again as the other women appear. Apparently, some of them are at another tribe, also coupled up with their Braxian warriors. I feel like I've entered the twilight zone. I imagined that these women were working their butts off to get off this planet, but most of them seem more than content to stay.

Dragix is silent next to me, but he tenses each time one of the Braxians comes close. I stroke my thumb over his hand, and he tolerates the men, but I can tell he's not happy.

"How'd you escape the dragon?" Nevada asks. "And who's this guy?"

This is awkward. I glance at Dragix. We didn't discuss

whether he wants everyone to know what he is. And that he has a more vulnerable form. My head is spinning at everything that's happening, and I take a moment to think.

Nevada is standing next to a Braxian who introduced himself as the tribe king, Rakiz. He wraps an arm around her, and she smiles up at him before returning her attention to me.

I suddenly don't feel comfortable allowing these strangers to know Dragix's secret.

"Uh, he's, uh, a friend."

The look he gives me is not pleased, and out the corner of my eye, I catch the other women glancing at each other doubtfully.

I haven't attempted to use our mental pathway while Dragix is in this form, but I try anyway.

"I'm guessing you don't want them to know what you are." I stare at him, hoping he's picking up what I'm sending. I'm aware that I'm being unforgivingly rude and likely still look constipated with the effort it takes to send my message as the other women watch. *"If you want to go now, it's okay. As you can see, I'll be fine."*

I give him a shaky smile, and he studies my face. Then he shakes his head.

"I am Dragix," he says. "And Charlie is under my protection. Anyone who harms her will answer to me."

Zocy frowns at that. She's a small woman, about my height, and she's standing alone while a Braxian warrior hovers near her, occasionally glancing at us but always returning his gaze to her face. "I'm not sure I understand," she says softly.

"It's a bit crazy," I admit. "I'd never have believed it if I hadn't seen it for myself. But there you go."

Dragix shifts on his feet, a slow roll of his muscles.

Suddenly, it's clear that he may have been pretending to be unthreatening, but in reality, he's the biggest threat here.

The Braxians are instantly alert, studying Dragix as if they're weighing up killing him now.

Shit.

I did this. I let them see that he has a more vulnerable form.

I step in front of him, glaring at Rakiz. Nevada seems to find this amusing because I can see her grinning out the corner of my eye.

"Not only is Dragix the only remaining dragon after *your people* slaughtered his family, but he is my friend. If anyone here even thinks about hurting him, I swear I'll make them pay."

I glance around, meeting the eyes of every warrior around us. More have joined us, obviously drawn to the tense group who are currently staring at me as if I have two heads.

The warriors don't exactly look scared at my threat. That's okay. I'll still kill them if they hurt him.

I blink at that. I'm a pacifist. Other than Ben, I've never thought about hurting anyone in my life. But for Dragix...for Dragix, I'd burn this whole world to the ground if I had to.

"I am...your friend?"

"Of course, Dragix. You're more than that. You know that."

He's silent for a long moment as everyone around us gets tenser. *"I haven't had a friend since..."*

Since his family was slaughtered. By these people. Oh, I know it wasn't *these* Braxians. But I never should have brought him here, amongst people who have always been his enemies.

"You know what," I say, "this is a mistake. I shouldn't have come here."

"Wait," Ellie says. "It's just a lot to take in, Charlie." Her voice is low and soothing, and I realize I'm acting like a crazy person. But I won't allow these warriors to look at Dragix like they're wondering how difficult it would be to kill him.

It's not that they necessarily want him dead. I can tell by the way the Braxians are slowly shifting their bodies so that the women are behind them. They think they need to protect the human women from him.

The problem is that Dragix has always been the bogeyman to these guys. The huge beast flying overhead. Now I've shown them that he has a much more vulnerable form.

"I need you to shift."

Dragix turns his gaze to me. He doesn't look at all worried. Maybe that's why the Braxians are acting like he's a threat. He's surrounded by enemies, and he's as cool as a cucumber, safe in the knowledge that he could kill them all in seconds.

The only way to resolve this is to make them see that he's not prey. That he *could* easily kill them but he's choosing not to. Because if they ever do attack him, even if they think that they're doing it to protect their women, Dragix will turn this place to ash.

"They will be frightened. Is this what you want?"

"They're not frightened enough right now. They're spooked, but they're wondering if they can kill you before you shift forms. I want them to see that you came here in your most vulnerable form and didn't attack. That you can either be an ally or an enemy."

"This will make it difficult for the other females to trust you."

"I don't care."

His gaze is steady on my face, and then he finally nods.

"You guys need to back up," I say aloud. "You don't believe this is Dragix? He's going to prove it."

"It's okay," Ellie soothes. "We believe you, Charlie."

I shake my head. "Your warriors are already reaching for weapons, wondering if they can kill him before he shifts. Maybe they need to see how fast that shift happens."

"Charlie," Nevada says, and her face is pale. I ignore her and turn to Dragix.

In the blink of an eye, he's a dragon. People stumble back, and the entire camp comes to a halt. Swords are drawn, and I step in front of him.

"Move, little two-leg. They cannot hurt me in this form. Their swords will not penetrate my scales. But I do not like you shielding me." His voice is gentle, soothing, and my eyes heat. What's wrong with me? I've somehow made this entire situation worse.

His shift was faster than I've ever seen it. I didn't realize he could shift within a second, and I'm guessing he had to reach deep to do it.

Dragix runs his gaze over every face around us. The air is tense with fear, the women pale as they stare at him. The Braxians are baring their teeth, ready for his attack.

He lies down, curling up like a cat. He even places his head on the ground, looking for all the world like he's about to take a nap.

Some of the tension eases.

"Were you expecting him to slaughter you all?" I ask, eyeing the Braxians, the swords still in their hands.

"That's enough," Nevada tells me, elbowing Rakiz aside. He growls at her but allows her to step closer. "I understand that you're feeling protective of your huge, lethal dragon, but you need to take it down a notch. This is a giant predator. One that you have brought to our home. These men are simply reacting to the threat."

"He's not a threat."

"And how would we know that?" Nevada smiles at me, but her eyes are serious. "Let's all take a moment here. The dragon—Dragix," she says as my eyes narrow, "is obviously chill. So let's all relax and put up our swords, hmm?"

My eyebrows shoot up as the warriors all obey her. Dragix moves behind me, raising his head, and I stroke a hand down his snout.

"I'm...sorry," I apologize to everyone, my cheeks heating. "It's just...Dragix has kept me safe. He's not some ravaging monster who's going to kill you all. You're right. I was feeling overprotective."

Zoey smiles at me, but it's Nevada that steps closer.

"Men can make even the most logical women lose their damn minds," she says. "I get it. Now that we've all cooled down a little, welcome home." She hugs me, and I finally relax, hugging her back.

CHAPTER TWELVE

C harlie

Dragix follows me into the tent that Nevada refers to as a kradi. It's large and welcoming, and I slump down on one of the many huge pillows on the floor. Dragix lounges next to me. His pants tore into shreds when he shifted, and I reach for a pillow, placing it in his lap.

He gives me a look but allows it.

Ellie walks in, smiling at me. "Are you guys hungry?"

I shake my head, but she gestures to a long table against one of the kradi's "walls."

"Help yourself if you feel peckish."

She sits down and examines me, and I examine her back.

"So," I say, curious as hell. "You're pregnant, huh?"

Ellie bursts out laughing. "I sure am." She holds out her arms, displaying gorgeous bracelets that look like woven gold threads. "These are mating bands. They mean that I'm basically married to Terex."

"Congratulations. So you're not planning to leave?"

She shakes her head, and I examine the women who have arrived while we were talking. Ellie isn't the only one with the gold bands—I can see some on Nevada's wrists as well, and I saw gold glinting on Ivy's arms when she was cuddled up with a grim-faced warrior earlier. He looked like he wanted to kill something until he gazed at Ivy, and his face softened into something like adoration.

"I am," one of the women says, and I glance at her. "I'm Vivian. I'm planning to get off this planet. So is Zoey."

I raise my eyebrow at Zoey, and she stares back at me. She's the one who the huge warrior was hovering around earlier. She nods silently, and I glance at the others.

"Anyone else?"

Nevada shifts, drawing my attention to her. "Alexis is mated to Dexar, another tribe king. They were supposed to be here earlier, but they're obviously running late. Beth is coming with them, along with Zarix. We've been planning this meeting for a while, so it's great that you happened to arrive today." Her eyes shift to Dragix, and I reach for his hand. She smiles faintly, and then we all turn as someone steps into the kradi.

"Hello, hello!" Alexis looks like she was born to wear the gauzy mint-colored dress that clings to her body, swirling around her ankles. Behind her, a woman I don't recognize steps gracefully into the tent, her movements like she's floating on air. By process of elimination, I'm guessing that this is Beth.

"Charlie!" Alexis says. "It's so good to see you. And who is this?"

I open my mouth, but it's my dragon who speaks. "Dragix," he says, and Alexis blinks.

She stares at him. "I recognize your eyes," she says softly. "From when we saw you by the river."

He nods, and she gives him a wide grin.

"If you're on our side, we could really use some help moving that ship in the river."

I frown at that. "How come?"

"There's a chance that the fluid leaking from it may be responsible for the low birth rates of female babies amongst the Braxians."

Dragix is tense and quiet next to me, and I can practically hear him thinking that it would be a good thing if the Braxians were to die out naturally.

The silence stretches, turning to awkwardness, and I sigh. "How about we figure out what do with those purple aliens if they really are returning?"

Alexis nods. "That's why we're late," she says. "We decided to check out the ship on the way here."

"And?" Nevada asks, her eyes sharp.

Alexis blows out a shaky breath. "And it's no longer flashing at all. The light is just continually red."

I pull another pillow close and hug it to me. "What does that mean?"

"I think it means that they're almost here. I'd bet money that it's some kind of beacon, and I think that their ship is so close that they could be here any day."

We're all silent at that. I glance at Dragix, and he's staring at the kradi entrance, his mind obviously elsewhere.

If they really are returning, we need to be prepared. "Okay," I say. "What are we going to do about it?"

Nevada sits up. "Rakiz and Dexar are working with some of the other tribes, attempting to convince them to help us fight. The problem is that they don't have any real reason to put everything on the line for us. There aren't any human women at risk in their tribes."

Beth clears her throat. "A few of the other tribes have agreed to fight as part of their alliance, but they're not happy about it."

I frown. "We need to convince the other tribes that they'd be at risk too. If these aliens are returning, it's likely that they're going to take a look around and grab anything they find interesting, right? Who's to say they wouldn't take the Braxian women?"

Ellie nods. "That's what we're trying to tell them."

Ivy speaks up. "I think we need to go across the water and talk to the king on the other side."

I raise my eyebrow at that, my mouth dropping open as she explains how she was kidnapped by the Zintas and taken across the Colossal Water to an actual city. Maybe this planet isn't as undeveloped as I thought.

"What would make him want to help us?" Nevada asks. "He didn't seem to give two craps that you'd been kidnapped, and then he showed up just in time to tell us to fuck off."

Ivy chews her lip at that and shrugs.

We're all silent for a long moment, depressed.

Ellie gets to her feet. "I'm sure you guys are tired from traveling. Why don't we settle in and meet again tomorrow morning? We can brainstorm overnight and discuss our ideas when we're feeling fresher."

The other women nod and change the subject, some of them filing out of the kradi. Nevada makes her way over to us.

"I've had a kradi set up for you guys," she says, and Dragix stiffens next to me. "I'll show you where it is."

We follow her out of the kradi, and Dragix freezes as he stares at the Braxian next to Beth. The Braxian is smiling down at her, and Dragix shakes next to me, the rage pouring off him in waves.

"What is it, Dragix?"

"That male. He looks exactly like the Braxian who killed my sister."

I flinch at the banked rage in his voice.

Nevada is standing next to us, her expression puzzled. "Do you know Zarix?"

Dragix stares at Zarix silently and I can see death in his eyes. I never should have brought him here. Never should have asked him to stay. This is a special kind of torture for him.

"No," he says finally, turning away, and Nevada frowns at him and but shrugs, leading us to our kradi.

* * *

Dragix

I must leave this place. Everything about these people makes me feel on edge. That Braxian...he looked so much like the male who killed Ezra. The one who speared her with his fire stick when she was too weak to fight back.

If I stay here...I fear I will kill them all.

"Will you stay with me tonight?" Charlie asks softly, and I study her beautiful face. I should go. But I find I cannot leave without one more night with her. One more night of stroking her soft skin, kissing her lush mouth, losing myself in her incredible body. One more night of her hands on me, her blue eyes gazing up at me like I hold the answers to all of her questions.

"I will stay tonight."

She nods, giving me a trembling smile. "This is goodbye, isn't it?"

"It was always goodbye, little two-leg. You will be safe here."

She nods again but not like she accepts my words. She is still considering some way to convince me to stay for longer. She opens her mouth, and I lean down, pleased as her lips soften under mine, her mouth opening.

I lift her into my arms and take her to the large pile of furs in the corner of the structure the Braxians refer to as a kradi. I may not want to be in this place with these people, but I can acknowledge that they have provided Charlie with comfort and warmth.

I gently lay her down on the furs and stare down at her flushed face.

Suddenly, I want to howl. To roar. To ask her why she would want to stay here with these two-legs. Why she won't instead come back with me. But she wishes to be with the other females of her kind. Wishes to fight against the purple males who think to take her on their metal ships.

I growl at that, and Charlie blinks up at me. I have become too close to my little two-leg. When I leave here tomorrow, I must force myself to stay away. Otherwise, I fear that I will take her with me, chain her to me for the rest of her days.

Already, what I feared the most has happened. My immortality has drained away to almost nothing. If I do not leave tomorrow and revert back to my winged form, I will... die. I knew—when the Zintas attacked and managed to wound me—that I was becoming weak. That I risked losing my extended life span. And I stayed in two-leg form anyway.

So I could spend more time with Charlie. I stare down at her and force myself to use my logic.

I am the last of my people. When I die, we are gone. Forever. The Braxians will have succeeded in eradicating us. I will never let that happen. Once I have said goodbye to Charlie, I will stay in winged form for the rest of my life, if that's what it takes.

Charlie's blue eyes are examining my face. "What is it?"

"Let us not talk now. Let us be together."

She frowns at that, and I reach down, brushing my thumb over the soft lines between her brows, smoothing them away. Then I take her mouth, delving deep as I run my hands up her body, desperate to touch every inch of her skin, to *imprint* myself on her.

I may be leaving her, but I will ensure that she will never forget me.

She makes soft, urgent sounds beneath me as I move my mouth from hers and trail it down her neck. I breathe in her scent, and just like that I'm ravenous for her as I pull her tunic over her head.

Gods. She is so soft, so smooth, her breasts fitting perfectly in my hands. I squeeze them gently and then brush my thumbs over her nipples. She shudders, her head falling back, her eyes blurred, and I do it again. And again.

"Dragix..."

Her voice is a plea, and I can't deny her. She wriggles out of her pants, and within moments, my own clothes are in a pile next to hers.

If this is the last time I will touch my little two-leg, I will make the most of it. I will go slow, memorize the feel of her.

Her hand slides down, clamping around me, and I see stars.

She laughs at my low growl, and any thoughts I had of drawing this out are immediately pushed from my mind.

I feel a savage need to pound into her, to mark her as mine. To make it so that no other male will ever compare to what I can do to her.

The idea of another male touching her is enough to make me snarl, and Charlie's eyes widen. But I am large, and I would never hurt my tiny female.

I slide my hand down and gently brush against the small nub of nerves that makes her moan. I push one finger inside her, watching as her eyes flutter shut.

"I need to be inside you," I murmur.

"Yes. Inside me now," she says, twisting her hips against my hand.

I replace my hand with my cock, pressing it against her. Then I'm pressing into her as she whimpers, angling her hips so I can slide deeper.

I sink in, harder than I've ever been, groaning at the heat of her as she squeezes around me. And then I'm deep within her, pelvis to pelvis, and she meets my gaze with a moan.

I begin to thrust, her walls gripping me, and I fist her curly hair, kissing her the way she taught me, thrusting my tongue deep and claiming her mouth.

My hands slide to her hips, holding them steady as I pound deep, ravishing her as she tightens even more around me, throwing her head back.

Her breath catches, and I slam my mouth down on hers, capturing her loud groans as she shakes and trembles around me. I follow her over, pleasure bursting along my every nerve, my limbs trembling as I claim her one last time.

How will I make myself leave her?

Charlie

Dragix brushes a gentle kiss to my cheek, and the furs rustle around me as he gets out of bed.

I open my eyes. "Where are you going?"

His expression is resigned, and I narrow my eyes at him.

"You're leaving, aren't you? You were just going to sneak out of here without even saying goodbye."

"I thought it would be easier this way. For both of us."

I let out a choked laugh. "Easier? I never thought you were a coward, Dragix."

His eyes sharpen at that. But his expression is remote now, as if he has mentally already left.

I throw back the furs and get to my feet, ignoring the fact that I'm butt naked.

Dragix's eyes travel down my body before he wrestles them back to my face. "Be careful, little two-leg."

I stare at him. "You're threatening me now?"

"I am the one being that the warriors here fear. You should remember that."

"Fuck you." He steps forward, eyes flaring, and I hold up a hand. "Why are you picking a fight? So it'll be easier to leave me that way?" He's silent, and I laugh. "Right. You don't have to go, you know. You could stay here. With me. Help us fight off whatever is coming. *Be* with me, Dragix."

I'm practically begging, and his face is getting colder and more remote by the second. After last night...the thought of not seeing him again...it cracks something inside me.

"I don't belong here," he says. "These are not my people."

"I know they're not. But...they could be your people. At least for a little while."

He bares his teeth at that, and I realize it was the worst

thing I could have said. He turns and stalks from the kradi, and I pull on a pair of pants, cursing as I shove my legs into them.

Surprisingly, he hasn't flown away by the time I stumble from the kradi, still pulling my shirt over my head. He's stalking toward the camp gates, ignoring the few Braxians who are walking through the camp this early.

The sun is rising, bathing the ground with a warm light. The air is cool and fresh, and my heart is breaking.

I follow him, running to catch up with his long stride. And then I push him behind one of the kradis. It's only the fact that I have surprise on my side that makes it work, and he blinks at me for a moment before his face hardens again.

"The people here could die, Dragix."

He's silent, and I stare at him.

"You don't care, do you?"

"I told you. I only care about you."

I've made a mistake giving him human traits. Imagining that he felt human emotions. He'll never be able to see past his rage and hurt to help the Braxians, even if it means also helping me and the other women.

I step back. I've made a fool of myself chasing after him. We agreed to this. He was going to drop me off here and leave. I'm the one who asked him to stay the night.

My mistake.

He looks at me, those gold eyes hard. But something flickers in them as we stare at each other, and his mouth tightens, as if he's fighting back the words he wants to say.

I clear my throat. I did what I swore I would never do again. I got attached to a man who I knew would hurt me. It may not be physical pain, but it still feels agonizing enough to kill me.

"There's no point drawing this out, then." I step back. "Goodbye, Dragix."

He nods, his face blank. But I know him well enough by now to see torment flash through those gold eyes.

"Goodbye Charlie."

CHAPTER THIRTEEN

C harlie

I feel like I've been cut open and left to bleed out. But I put on a happy face and attempt to explain why Dragix chose not to help us.

It's obvious that the other women don't understand, but they accept my explanations anyway. We have bigger things to worry about, and after another meeting, we've decided that some of us will travel to the tribes that still haven't agreed to ally with us.

Tomorrow, I'll be heading to a tribe that's located close to what the others call the Colossal Water. Apparently, the tribe king is called Khax. His tribe hasn't been seen for a while and has only recently returned to this area. Rakiz described Khax's warriors as savages, which, given how brutal *these* warriors are in their training arena, makes me more than a little nervous.

But we need allies. I can vividly remember the long

sticks that the aliens used to shock us. If they have other weapons like that, we need to find a way to disable them before they use them on us.

The Braxians are tough sons of bitches, but they're still only armed with swords and crossbows.

I bring my attention back to the present as Ivy touches my knee.

"How are you doing?" she asks gently.

My eyes sting, and I push the palms of my hands against them. We're sitting in the same kradi as yesterday, only the others have already wandered off to do whatever they need to do. Zoey is crushing some kind of sweet-smelling herbs in the corner, and she sends me a sympathetic look as I move my hands away from my face.

"I'm...struggling," I admit. "Who would've thought that I'd fall for the dragon who kidnapped me and took me back to his lair? It's like something out of a bad fairy tale."

Zoey grins at me from across the room. "You know, the original fairy tales are much worse than the soft little stories we were told as kids. If it was really a bad fairy tale, the dragon would have eaten you and used your bones to pick your flesh out of his teeth."

Ivy and I both stare at her, and she blushes.

"Sorry," she mutters, and we crack up.

It feels good to laugh about something, anything.

"He's basically a sociopath," I mutter. "He doesn't care about anyone but me, and even that seems iffy right now."

Ivy tilts her head. "You've been trying to treat him like he's human."

I shrug. Her words echo what I was thinking earlier. Dragix isn't human. I *know* that. But still... "I have. And I've been alone for so long. My ex...he was abusive. It was bad. And I don't think he ever truly loved me. I don't think he knew *how* to love. I was young and lonely, mourning my family, and he wanted me because I fulfilled a purpose. Someone to dominate. To hurt. When Dragix took me, one of the first things he said was, 'I saw you, and I took you. I am Dragix. I can do what I like.'" Tears are running down my face, and I brush at them. Across the kradi, Zoey's eyes are wet in sympathy, and Ivy puts her arm around me.

"You think they're the same."

"Yes…no…I don't know."

"Did Dragix ever…hurt you?"

"No. Never. He was obsessed with healing me actually. When we first met, he was little more than a beast. But he was still careful with me. I just…I worry that *I'm* the problem. That I'm only interested in emotionally unavailable, possessive men."

Ivy tilts her head. "I get it, but two guys is not a pattern. You can't compare an abusive jackass on Earth with an alien dragon on Agron. I know it's tempting to try and 'figure it out' so that it'll hurt less. But do you think blaming yourself and putting Dragix in the same category as your ex will make you feel better?"

"No. No, not at all. I just miss him. Life was simple on that mountain, you know?"

She nods. "I get it. Men suck."

Zoey and I both laugh, but Ivy's face is serious, although her eyes sparkle.

"I get what it's like to fall for a guy who's considered barbaric even on *this* planet, which truly takes some work. Vrex was living his life as a hermit in the woods before I managed to civilize him."

She grins at us, and she looks so happy, so content, that I'm suddenly wrestling with envy, wishing with everything I have that Dragix was with me right now.

The grin disappears, and she squeezes my hand. "It'll get better, I promise. It'll just take time. Thankfully, you have more than enough stuff to distract you right now."

I laugh. "That's for sure. Any advice for talking to this tribe tomorrow?"

"Don't let them intimidate you. Stay cool and lay out exactly what it will mean for *them* if those purple bastards are given free rein on this planet."

I nod, and we watch while Zoey transfers her herbs to a small wooden bowl. She has mostly been quiet, her mind obviously elsewhere, and she glances at me.

"I wish I could come with you."

"You can," I say, surprised. I hadn't thought she wanted to come.

She shakes her head. "Tagiz will lose his mind."

Ivy glances at me and then narrows her eyes at Zoey. "Is he bossing you around, girl? You know you can't let these warriors get away with that shit. If they thought we'd take it, they'd keep us tucked up safe in our kradis day and night."

I laugh at the thought, and Ivy grins at me. Then she returns her attention to Zoey, who blushes.

"It's not that. I mean...he's definitely bossy, but I think that's in the Braxian blood. It's just that...he's the one who rescued me, and he seems to think it's his responsibility to make sure I'm safe every moment of every day. He treats me like a *patient*."

Zoey's lower lip sticks out in a pout, and her huge eyes are wide with annoyance. She has lost weight since I saw her last, and her sharp collarbones and high cheekbones make her look fragile. Her skin is pale and flawless, with a few tiny freckles scattered across her small nose, and her dark hair is tousled around her shoulders.

"Well," I say, "unfortunately you suffer from terminal cuteness."

Zoey glares at me, and I laugh.

"Girl, I was the smallest kid in my class my whole life, I get it."

Ivy chimes in, "Add in the fact that you almost died in front of Tagiz, and he's likely struggling with all those instincts that make Braxians so good in bed but so much work to deal with out of the furs. Even a human guy would want to look after you, but you're going to have to show him that you don't need him to baby you."

"How do I do that?" Zoey wails, and I stare at her.

"This is a lot of drama for a random Braxian. Spill."

She turns bright pink and chews on her lower lip. "I kissed him," she admits.

"Oooh, girl," Ivy crows. "I knew you had it in you."

Zoey is now bright red. "I was proud of myself too until he pushed me away and told me he didn't want to *hurt* me."

Yikes.

"There's only one thing for it," I say, and Zoey angles her head. "Prove to him that you're better. But you can't do that until you actually are better. If you push yourself too much and end up passing out or something, you'll just prove him right."

Ivy nods. "In the meantime, if you want him to stop seeing you as a patient, you need to ban any conversations about your health," she says. "That's what I'd do anyway. Only talk to him if it's about something else and he'll soon get the message."

Zoey blinks, and then her eyes harden. "You're right. I'm a nurse. I deal with pushy doctors and difficult patients all damn day. I can handle one Braxian male."

Ivy grins and shoots me a look, and I laugh. I can't wait to see the fireworks.

"That's the spirit," Ivy says.

Dragix

I can feel Charlie like a ghost inside me. My little two-leg is in my blood, in the air I breathe. Everything reminds me of her, from the forest she liked to explore, to the river she once bathed in naked.

Even basking in the sun on top of my mountain holds no pleasure. I keep opening one eye, expecting to see Charlie sauntering out of my lair, a grin on her face as she pleads with me to take her flying.

Maez walks up the stairs and sits next to me, staring out over the plains below.

"It's quiet around here without Charlie," she says, ignoring me as I snarl at her.

"She belongs with the other two-legs."

"And you? Where do you belong, Dragix?"

"Here." Alone. For eternity.

Maez's dark eyes are on me, and I show her the edges of my teeth. She rolls her eyes, something I never saw her do until Charlie was with us, constantly demonstrating her irreverence.

The sight reminds me so much of Charlie—of the way she would tease me, hoping to make me growl so she could laugh in delight—that I can no longer even look at Maez.

I get to my feet, ignoring her sigh as I spread my wings and leave my mountain behind.

I fly over my territory, absently scanning it for Zintas,

Braxians, or a beautiful, dark-haired female making her way back to me.

I push the thought aside and bank left, swooping down to hunt. Then I make my way to the river, where Charlie first saw the other two-leg female.

If I had never allowed her to leave my lair, she would not have talked to the others. They would have imagined her dead, would have left us alone. Eventually, Charlie would have accepted her fate. She would have stayed with me.

That would make me no better than the male who caused her such pain and suffering.

I glower at the large ship, half sunk in the river. The idea of a solution to whatever fertility problems the Braxians have...it is not a good thought. It does not please me at all. I would be happy if they died out naturally. Surely even my mother would not expect me to actively help the Braxian race prosper.

I land in the river, studying the ship. Then I'm the one mentally rolling my eyes at myself as I push against it. I am strong, but the ship has been stuck here for decades. I use my claws to scrape at the riverbed, to push the rocks aside, and then I dig in, pushing against the ship again with a roar.

I push until it sits on the riverbank, no longer contaminating the water—if that is indeed the source of the Braxians' problems.

Perhaps...perhaps one day Charlie will see this. And maybe she will know that even if I could not stay with her, could not surround myself with my enemies, I am not a monster.

A thought occurs to me, one so repulsive that I roar, flames surrounding me as I lose control.

Charlie is beautiful and brave, and she...shines. Braxian males will fight to win her. If she does not find her way home to her planet, she will eventually mate with one of them. They will have younglings.

I eye the ship. Perhaps now they will be more likely to have daughters, with her soft, curly hair and dark-blue eyes.

It takes more self-control than I have ever used before not to push the ship back into the water. Not to set this world on fire. Not to fly to the Braxian camp and snatch Charlie up from where other males are likely sniffing around her.

I tremble with rage, and it is only the thought of her face and the disappointment in her eyes that keeps me from doing just that.

CHAPTER FOURTEEN

C harlie

We're leaving early this morning. Zoey was forced to admit that she's not yet up to the journey, even if she'd like to be. But from the way she was huddled and whispering with a warrior called Hewex earlier, it's obvious that she's up to something.

Good for her.

There's a lot riding on this visit. Rakiz is already away negotiating with another tribe, and apparently his ally Dexar—Alexis's mate—is doing the same. They'll return to camp later today, but for now, it's our turn to step up. They're trusting us to convince Khax—the king of a tribe they consider savages—to help us fight.

My eyes are heavy and gritty from a night of no sleep. From the sympathetic look Ellie just shot me, I don't need a mirror to know that they're likely swollen and red as well.

To say I miss Dragix is the understatement of the year. I wonder what he's doing now. If he's in our hot pools, flying over the forest, napping on top of his mountain. I wish...

That's enough of that.

I force my attention back to the present and smile at one of the Braxians who is coming with us. His name is Jozet, and he looks like his face would crack if he smiled back at me. He gestures to one of the slightly terrifying beasts they call "mishua," and I gulp as it stares at me through red eyes.

"She won't hurt you," Jozet says. "Her name is Vari."

"Vari, huh? Nice to meet you." I slowly raise my hand to her face, and when Jozet doesn't object, I stroke along her nose. Her scales are very different compared to Dragix's, but the feel of them beneath my hand still makes my throat tighten.

She gazes at me and lets out a tiny snort, but when I go to remove my hand, she nudges it, encouraging me to pat her some more.

I laugh. "Spoiled girl."

Jozet's face stays blank, but his eyes dance as he slaps her lightly on her flank. "They're all spoiled. They wouldn't tolerate anything less."

"Neither would I," an amused voice says, and I glance over my shoulder at Vivian.

"What are you doing up this early?"

"I'm coming with you."

Jozet sighs, and Vivian ignores him.

"I always get stuck behind," she tells me. "I'm desperate for some adventure."

I raise my eyebrow. Somehow, in a warrior camp on an alien planet, Vivian looks impeccable. She's done something to her eyes to darken her lashes, and her hair spills down her back like gold silk. Her dress fits like it has been tailored, but the steely look in her eye warns me that while she may care about her appearance, she's no airhead.

"If you're sure. Jozet said we need to travel fast if we're going to get back this afternoon. Otherwise, we'll have to camp somewhere."

Vivian sends me an amused look. "What are we waiting for?"

Jozet mutters something and stalks away to talk to another Braxian. They chat for a few moments, and then the other guy surveys Vivian before finally nodding.

"What's going on?" I ask.

"That's Duvix," she says. "He was going to be traveling with you guys anyway, and now Jozet is telling him he'll have to ride with me." She glances at me and rolls her eyes. "The mishua don't let women ride them. Just like everything else on this planet, they're as primitive as it comes."

The mishua glares at Vivian, and Vivian narrows her eyes back.

"Can they...understand you?"

"Who knows. Anyway, Duvix and Jozet are both still pissed at me. Back when we were still trying to find you guys, there was only one person who could be counted on to flirt with the Braxians for information. Information that Nevada needed so she would know where to look."

I can't help but smile. "And you were that person."

"That's right. I did what I needed to do to help—the only skill set I have, really." Her tone is self-deprecating, and I want to tell her not to talk shit about herself. But I sure don't know her well enough for that.

"So," she continues, "these guys got yelled at when Rakiz figured out who had spilled the most valuable information. They're still salty about it."

I eye her. "Let me guess, you don't exactly feel bad about their saltiness."

She shrugs. "They looked at me and saw an airhead who flirted with anyone who breathed. I taught them not to judge a book by its cover."

I grin as the warriors return, their expressions dark. "You know what, I think we're going to be good friends."

Vivian links her arm through mine as the men saddle up the mishua. "I think so too."

It doesn't take long before we're ready to go, and Jozet is a calming presence behind me once I'm seated on the mishua. He didn't say a word when I handed him my cloth sack, simply attaching it to the saddle before showing me where to hold on to the mishua.

The mishua's gait isn't anything like a horse's. It's bumpier, and without Jozet's arm around my waist, I'd likely tumble off Vari as she lurches along the path.

We're in the same forest that Dragix used to explore with me. Or at least, I'd explore, and he'd watch my face, smiling at my reactions. I keep glancing up at the sky, expecting to see him fly overhead, but he's obviously either back on his mountain or hunting somewhere else.

The sun is soon high in the sky, and we don't bother stopping for lunch. Jozet hands me a waterskin and some dried meat, and I munch as we leave the cool shade of the forest for a wide, open plain.

The warriors are on high alert, and it makes me jumpy. I constantly scan our surroundings, wishing I was wearing a pair of shorts and a tank top as beads of sweat roll down my neck. It's humid today, and I can practically feel my hair expanding, while Vivian somehow still looks great. Her face is flushed, but she looks like she's been playing tennis on an indoor, air-conditioned court.

I narrow my eyes at her as Jozet and Duvix draw their mishua close so they can talk.

"I could learn to hate you," I say, and she bursts out laughing.

If Dragix were here, he'd give me a slow grin and peel off my clothes. He loved my hair wild and would spend hours playing with my curls as we talked.

"You've got that look on your face again," Vivian says.

I open my mouth to reply, but the mishua begin walking up a hill, and I clutch at one of Vari's horns.

As soon as we're at the top of the hill, a group of Braxians appear, swords in their hands.

"We are here to speak to Khax," Jozet says. "It is of vital importance."

The warriors study us, murmuring amongst themselves.

"Hand over your weapons," they say, and Jozet snorts.

"We have been tasked with protecting these females," he says.

One of the other warriors bares his teeth. "You imply that we would hurt females?"

This is going well.

Vivian stretches, the movement drawing the attention of every male eye as it highlights her impressive breasts and tiny waist.

"I'd love to get off this mishua," she purrs. "Surely you don't expect our protectors to leave us completely defenseless, do you?"

I somehow manage to keep from smiling. In the past few hours, I've learned that Vivian is many things, but defenseless will never be one of them. Beneath the gorgeous face is a quick mind and a ruthless commitment to doing whatever needs to be done.

Before today, I wouldn't have chosen Vivian if I needed

someone at my back. Even I was guilty of judging her by her appearance.

The warriors hesitate and then glance at me. I give them what I hope is a flirtatious smile, but I'm well aware that I'll never have one ounce of Vivian's sexual self-assurance.

"Fine," the first warrior says gruffly. They turn to walk away, and Jozet looks at Vivian and snorts.

"Do you have something you'd like to say?" she asks sweetly.

He shakes his head, and we clomp toward the camp.

I nibble at my lip until we enter the camp gates. One of the warriors points at a mishua pen, and we dismount, handing the mishua over to a group of warriors who take them from us.

"Wait," I say. "Can you please pass me that bag?"

Jozet hands it to me, and then we trail after the warriors who met us at the camp entrance.

It's clear that this camp is much more temporary than the camp we just came from. While Rakiz and Nevada share a tashiv—a hut also used for meetings—there's no such structure here. And while the kradis in Rakiz's camp are aligned in neat rows, the kradis here have been placed seemingly without rhyme or reason, so we're forced to dodge around them as we follow the warriors.

These Braxians are wearing knee-length loincloths, each with a long split up the side, and little else. They look dangerous, mean, and unfriendly as we walk through their camp with Jozet and Duvix.

They take us to a large communal area. Tribe members are sitting on rocks around a firepit, which, thanks to the current warm temperature, is unlit. The tribe members are facing a huge boulder, which has been hollowed out in a vague approximation of a throne.

There are absolutely no women here, I realize. We passed a few of them on the way through the camp, their eyes wide and curious, but this gathering is obviously some kind of men's club.

Awesome.

A Braxian lounges on the throne. His face is hard, and his nose has obviously been broken once or twice. He's the first Braxian I've ever seen with a full beard, and I can't help but stare. I'm guessing this is Khax.

"Strange females," he booms. "Where do you come from?"

Vivian steps forward and explains just how we got here and why we need his help. I keep my eyes on Khax, and I'm relieved to see a hint of interest on his face as she tells him about our situation.

He shifts on his throne. "And you are hoping to benefit from our reputation in battle."

I blink at that. Truthfully, Nevada said they were vicious savages and it would be great to get them on our side. She said nothing about the tribe's reputation.

Vivian doesn't miss a beat. "That's right," she says, giving him a sweet smile.

He snorts, but stares at us consideringly. "We are not the type to ally with tribes like Rakiz's," he says finally. "In fact, we have never sought any type of alliance with the Braxian tribes on this part of Agron."

I clear my throat. "And have you benefited from this insular approach? Or do you think it's possible that allying with Rakiz's tribe could lead to opportunities for your tribe?"

He scowls at that. "We have everything we need."

His jaw is hard, and I glance around, finding his warriors

leering at us. Vivian sighs but glances at me with a shrug. She's all out of ideas.

I hesitate, but I have one last card to play. I lift up my cloth sack, and he raises his eyebrow at me as I approach him. It breaks my heart to hold out the bundle, and my hand shakes. One of his guards steps forward, but Khax holds up his hand and reaches for it.

In spite of my devastation, I have to smile as he looks inside and his mouth drops open. He meets my eyes, and I force myself to speak around the lump in my throat.

"A gesture of good faith," I say. "We would love to have your support."

He pulls out one of Dragix's scales, and I clasp my hands together so I won't reach for it and snatch it away from him. It glimmers, a gorgeous aqua in the sunlight, but the next one he pulls out could be a deep forest green or a midnight blue.

Tribe members are murmuring at the sight of the scale.

"I would be interested to know how you came to have these in your possession," Khax says.

I give him a bland smile. "That is a story for another day." He stares at me, and I keep my mouth shut. He doesn't get that piece of me.

Finally, he gives us a slow nod. I don't know what that nod means, but I force myself to turn, and we file out of the clearing.

I clamp my mouth shut as we make our way back to the mishua, Jozet and Duvix a threatening presence by our sides.

Vivian nudges me. "Are you sure about giving up those scales?"

"Yes." *No.* She gives me a look, and I sigh. "It's done now. Plus, Rakiz said this tribe is known for their strategies in battle. If Khax is the difference between us winning the war or ending up prisoners again, it's worth it."

She nods, and Jozet helps me up onto the mishua. I still have one precious scale tucked beneath my pillow. It's a gorgeous silvery blue that reminds me of the sun shining on those scales while he napped on the top of his mountain.

The next couple of hours pass quickly, all of us lost in our own thoughts. Since we left so early and our chat with Khax wasn't exactly lengthy, we arrive back at camp by midafternoon.

Nevada is waiting for us when we slide off the mishua. "Rakiz is in a meeting with Dexar and some of the other tribe kings. We've had some...news."

From the sick look on her face, I'm guessing that this isn't good news.

Vivian frowns. "What happened?"

"They're here. Our scouts spotted them near the forest close to camp. They're guarding their ship, but the rest of them seem to be spreading out and hunting. For us."

Oh God. I wipe my sweaty hands on my pants. "How the hell did they land without anyone noticing?"

Nevada shrugs. "Dead of the night. One of Dexar's sentries noticed some strange lights and reported it. When Dexar sent scouts back to the area..."

"What?"

"The aliens attacked. They killed two of the scouts. One of them was wounded but managed to get back to camp and warn Dexar."

I stare at her. "They know that we know they're here."

Nevada nods, and for the first time, she looks exhausted.

Vivian steps closer and rubs her arm. "Why don't you get some rest?"

Nevada shakes her head. "There's something else. Alexis

and Beth have both been putting off their mating ceremonies. They wanted to wait until we were all together." Guilt hits me. If I didn't know about this threat, would I have even left Dragix? I tune back in as Nevada continues, "As qatai and qatal, Alexis and Dexar should have a huge ceremony at their camp, but with this threat..."

I frown, not understanding. It's Vivian that seems to get it.

"They want to be mated in case Dexar goes down." Her voice is hollow.

Nevada nods, running a hand through her hair. She looks worn out, and I'm sure if Rakiz could see her right now, he'd be ordering her to rest.

Of course, she'd likely tell him exactly what he could do with that order. If there's one thing I've learned watching Nevada and Rakiz, it's that both of them are quick-tempered. But they're also quick to make up—constantly dragging each other into dark corners and stealing private moments whenever they can.

I had that—briefly—with Dragix. We had that passion, that...need.

"Charlie?"

"Sorry. I blanked. What difference will it make if Dexar...falls?"

Nevada sighs. "Alexis will be able to rule their tribe without him. At least in the short term. God, I can't believe we're even talking about this. What a shitshow."

Vivian sighs. "A shitshow is right. When is the ceremony?"

"Today. They thought it best to get it done. And then we plan for war."

I shiver as we follow Nevada to the kradi that Alexis has

been using with Dexar while she is here. She looks pale, but her eyes are hard and determined. Ivy, Beth, and Zoey are here, and from the looks on their faces, they haven't managed to cheer her up.

"How are you doing?" I ask, and she gives me a tiny smile.

"I'm fine. It's just...Dexar was so looking forward to this, to doing it properly in front of our tribe. He says we'll have another ceremony, but it's not the same. It shouldn't be like this," she finishes in a whisper.

I don't know what to say. She's right. It shouldn't be like this.

Beth steps closer and kneels at her feet. "Do you love him?"

"Of course."

"Then this is just a chance to show off that love to your family and friends. Don't let them steal this from you. Don't let them make it ugly."

A tear falls from Alexis's eye, and she wipes it away. "How'd you get so wise?"

Beth grins, and we all turn as Ellie walks in. Her bump seems larger today, and if she were on Earth, I'd say she was five or six months along. But that math sure doesn't work.

She smiles as she sees me looking. "Braxian babies are big," she says. "Moni says they also usually come earlier than our babies."

"Are you feeling okay?"

"Now that I'm not throwing up everything I eat, I feel great. I just can't wait to meet this little guy or girl." She glances at Alexis. "How do you feel about a sunset ceremony?"

Alexis smiles, and this time most of the sadness is gone.

"That sounds lovely. Tell my bossy Braxian that he's not allowed to see me before the ceremony. Some traditions are still sacred."

We all laugh, and for the next few hours, we talk about everything *but* the aliens who have just landed on Agron.

CHAPTER FIFTEEN

C harlie

Alexis looks incredible. Her long blonde hair has been swept up into an elegant updo, and her dress is an icy blue that perfectly matches her eyes.

Vivian did her makeup, which is apparently a tradition for mating ceremonies around here, and her lips are stained a deep cherry red while her eyes have been lightly lined with kohl.

On her head sits a crown, the shiny jewels glinting like they're on fire in the sun.

She's standing next to Dexar, and they only have eyes for each other as they speak the formal words that will cement their mating.

My chest is so tight it aches.

One of Dexar's warriors steps forward, and I fan my face. For some reason, a fire has been lit, and while the sun is setting, the temperature is still warm.

I frown as the warrior lifts Alexis into his arms and walks to the fire. I tense, and Nevada puts her hand on my arm.

"Shh," she murmurs. "Watch." She slides her hand down to her stomach, and my eyes widen as I realize she's also pregnant.

These Braxian warriors waste no time.

I return my attention to where Dexar is now standing on the opposite side of the fire, and then I'm gaping as the warrior throws Alexis into the air, high above the fire. She soars over the flames and lands in Dexar's arms, her smile blinding.

I glance at Nevada, and she grins at the look on my face. "Dexar's tribe doesn't do this, but when he heard about our tradition, he said it sounded like it represented his and Alexis's relationship."

I turn back to the happy couple. Alexis has her arms wrapped around Dexar's neck, and his mouth is on hers as they ignore the whoops of the crowd.

"That part is meant to come later," Nevada laughs.

Rakiz steps forward and murmurs something to Dexar, who pulls his mouth away from Alexis with a grin. Then he places her back on her feet and makes a show of pulling his hands off her, holding them up in the air.

The crowd laughs, and Rakiz hands him two golden bands.

"Lexi," Dexar says, and my eyes fill with tears at the pure *love* on his face. "These bands represent our bond. Strong, true, and never to be broken. Will you accept them?"

Alexis is crying now. "I will."

Dexar ties the bands around her wrists, and then Beth steps forward, handing Alexis her own bands.

Alexis smiles at him through her tears.

"Dexar," she says, her voice cracking, and she takes a shuddering breath. "These bands represent our bond. Strong, true, and never to be broken. Will you accept them?"

His green eyes are practically glowing as he nods.

"I will," he says solemnly, and she ties the bands around her warrior's wrists.

Nevada leans close to me. "With this act, she's telling everyone that she's his equal and he's hers, just as she's his," she murmurs.

"It's beautiful."

I brush more tears off my face, embarrassed. God, I'm losing it. Some of the reason is that the ceremony is lovely, and Dexar and Alexis are clearly so in love that their happiness practically shines like a beacon.

And part of it is that I so deeply miss my dragon that it's taking every ounce of my self-control not to turn on my heel and walk out of the camp gates, through the forest, and up the mountain until I find him.

I blink as I realize the ceremony is over, and then I line up with the other women to hug Alexis while the Braxians slap Dexar on the back. Rakiz is grinning like a fool as he examines Dexar's mating bands, obviously happy for his friend.

Alexis wraps her arms around me.

"Congratulations," I tell her, forcing myself to smile. "What happens now?"

She grins back at me, obviously ecstatic. "Now we eat, drink, and dance."

Tables have been set up around the clearing, and food appears as if out of thin air. This ceremony was a last-minute arrangement, yet you'd never know by the bunches of wildflowers sitting in tall wooden vases and the platters of food waiting for us to dig in.

I take my seat and can't help but laugh as someone begins playing an instrument similar to a violin and Beth drags her huge warrior onto the small area being used as dance floor. He looks exceedingly uncomfortable, but he gazes at her like she hung the moon and the stars as she wraps her arms around his neck and beams up at him.

One by one, couples pair off. Ellie is sitting on Terex's lap while he murmurs into her ear. Nevada is obviously teasing Rakiz because she elbows him in the gut and says something to him with a sly smile. He glances down at her, buries his hand in her hair, and takes her mouth in a kiss that has me fanning myself again.

Alexis and Dexar are still talking to well-wishers, although Dexar has his arm wrapped so tightly around her that it's like they're one person. She grins up at him, and the look he gives her is so tender that I have to glance away.

Even Zoey is dancing with her stone-faced warrior, although he insists on a slow, gentle swaying motion as she gives him an exasperated look.

And Ivy? Ivy is currently pressed against a tree on the very edge of the clearing, and I can see nothing but her arms around Vrex's waist as he leans down and kisses along her neck.

These warriors obviously have no problem with PDA.

"Nothing but love around here," Vivian murmurs, sitting next to me.

"How do you deal with it?"

She raises her eyebrow. "How do I deal with what? Being alone?"

I feel my cheeks heat. "That's not what I meant."

She laughs. "Well, first, I'm not currently pining for a guy who I lived with for several weeks, so that helps." She shoots me a meaningful look, and I sigh.

"I miss him. I look around at all these happy people, and I just want to find my way back to his mountain."

"So why don't you?"

I chew on my lip. "I guess...if he can't put his hatred for the Braxians aside and help us fight, then it doesn't matter. I miss him so much, but he said he doesn't belong here. And I'm not going to let those purple bastards win."

Vivian nibbles on her lip. "I saw the way he looked at you. It was like it was painful for him to look away. I'm sorry it didn't work out."

"Yeah. Me too."

***

Dragix

My family is buried on the east side of our mountain. Beneath trees that have stood here since my father was a youngling.

I never brought Charlie here. I'm not sure why. She would never have judged me for my grief.

Maez is kneeling by my mother's grave, and she looks up, her eyes widening in surprise at my presence. I don't know what it says about me that I do not come here. That I can't stand to see the place where my family rests without me.

I glance at where Maez has been gardening, tending the area and making sure it does not become unkempt.

Something I have never thought to do.

"So much time has passed that the very landscape here is different. And yet it still feels like I lost them yesterday."

Maez gets to her feet, brushing dirt off her dress. "Grief is like that. I don't think it ever truly leaves us. But if we're lucky, it can become muted. It will always be there, Dragix, but your family wouldn't want you to suffer like this."

"I got to live."

"Yes," she says. "You got to *live*. It's up to you what you do with that precious gift, but from the stories I've heard about your mother, she wouldn't want you to waste it. She'd want you to make the most of the years you have."

"I don't know how."

She gives me a sad smile. "You never mourned, did you? You grew from that tiny boy into a huge dragon, and you went almost feral so you wouldn't have to think about what you lost."

"It worked."

"It did. But it was a temporary measure. How are you to move on if you never truly grieve?"

"I don't want to move on."

"Moving on doesn't mean forgetting them. It means honoring their memories by living. By loving."

My gaze has dropped to the cool dirt beneath my feet, but I raise them at that. Maez sighs at whatever she sees on my face.

"You have not left this mountain in days. This is the first time I have seen you in this form." I shrug, and she sighs again. "There's something you should know."

***

Charlie

After the mating ceremony, I spent the night curled up in my kradi, clutching the last of Dragix's scales to my chest and sobbing.

I wish I had spent less time comparing him to Ben. I

wish I'd jumped him that night when we first kissed and I left, comparing him to my sociopath ex.

Dragix is nothing like Ben.

If he were, he never would've let me go.

All day, I kept glancing up at the sky, expecting to see his huge form coming closer and closer.

I kept expecting him to come for me. To announce that he would help us.

But it's not going to happen, and I need to move on with my life.

I roll out of the furs and brush the tears off my face. I will get over this. I'm resilient as fuck. It's one of my best qualities.

I need to get out of here. I need to go and do something. Yesterday's trip to Khax's tribe was a good distraction. Maybe I can find another way I can help that will also keep me busy.

I find Dexar and Rakiz arguing when I get to Rakiz's tashiv. Nevada and Alexis are eating in the corner, watching the show with amused expressions.

Dexar throws up his hands, glowering at Rakiz. "You heard what he said when we rescued Ivy. It was a clear threat. What happens if he decides to kill you or hold you hostage?"

Rakiz raises one eyebrow. "I'm honored that you're so concerned for my safety."

Dexar is not amused. "And your pregnant mate? What happens when you don't come back?"

Rakiz growls at that, taking a step toward Dexar. Behind them, Nevada shakes her head and shoves a handful of nuts into her mouth.

Alexis smirks. "If you guys are going to fight, can you at least take your shirts off first?"

They're all insane.

Rakiz turns and glowers at Alexis, and Dexar tenses.

"Watch yourself," he says very softly.

I step forward. "Uh, guys?"

Maybe I should've chosen a better time for this. Rakiz gives me an unfriendly look, and Nevada gets to her feet, stepping forward and elbowing him in the ribs.

"Ignore these barbarians," she says. "What's up, Charlie?"

"I was just wondering if I could help out at all. Do you need Vivian and I to travel to any other tribes?"

Dexar glances at Rakiz, and Rakiz shakes his head.

I frown. "What?"

"We're currently talking about traveling across the water to speak to the king. However, we know nothing about him and therefore couldn't guarantee your safety."

Nevada tilts her head. "You know, Charlie and Vivian could be a good option. That guy was a dick, but Braxians have a code of honor, right? He's much less likely to be an asshole if two females go. If either of you guys go, it's riskier."

I nod. "Let me go. I'll do it."

Rakiz snorts. "And what happens when your dragon discovers we sent you into danger?"

My chest tightens, and I clench my fist, fighting the urge to rub at it. "Dragix won't care. He left." Dexar laughs at that, and I glower at him. "Either way, it's my life. I don't see him here. Do you?"

Alexis's eyes shine with sympathy, and I glance away.

Rakiz turns to pace, sending me the occasional considering look. "We would have to send enough warriors with her to keep her safe without it looking like a show of force."

Dexar lifts his shoulders in an elegant shrug and then

moves to one of the chairs near the unlit fire, reaching out his hand to snag Alexis's wrist and pulling her onto his lap.

I narrow my eyes at Rakiz. "Do you think this guy could help? Could he really make a difference if he showed up?"

Rakiz nods. "I know little about him, but even a hundred of his warriors could be all we need to wipe out our enemies."

"Then it's settled. I'm going."

Rakiz frowns at that, and Nevada moves close, wrapping her arm around his waist. "It's a good idea, Rakiz. You're just mad 'cause you didn't think of it," she teases. He gives her an exasperated look but finally nods.

I let out a relieved sigh. I don't know why I need to do this so badly. Maybe it's because I spent so many weeks hiding out with Dragix while these guys were looking for me. Or maybe it's because I'm hoping to replace thoughts of Dragix with the adrenaline I'll feel on this mission.

Either way, it's happening.

"Do you think Vivian will want to go with you?" Nevada asks.

I nod. "I'd be surprised if she didn't. I'll go ask her now. When can we leave?"

Rakiz frowns, obviously still unhappy about this turn of events, but he must realize it's the best option.

"Today," he says. "If you're going to go, it has to be as soon as possible."

I nod. "I'll go get ready, then."

Vivian is still asleep in her kradi when I arrive. She lets out a long groan, finally rolling onto her back and opening one eye.

"How the hell do you look so good when you first wake up?"

She scowls at me. "Good genes. Why are you here at the crack of dawn?"

I laugh. "You want to come on another adventure?"

Her eyes light up with interest, and she reaches for a dress as I tell her my plan.

"Excellent," she says. "I heard all about the city across the water when Nevada and Ivy got back, and I was pissed I didn't get to see it myself."

I raise my eyebrow. "You're not scared?"

She snorts. "If we can handle the giant barbarian we dealt with yesterday, then we can handle one Braxian king with a stick up his butt."

I wince. "You know you've jinxed us now, right?"

Vivian laughs. "How bad can it be?"

CHAPTER SIXTEEN

C harlie

The water is rough. Apparently, the last time the warriors with us crossed, it was about as calm as a puddle. Today, Hewex is throwing up over the side of the boat. Even Vivian looks slightly green next to me.

We're now close enough to the shore that I can see other boats, and I stare as Jozet and Duvix tie up ours.

Hewex attempts to pull himself together while Tagiz says something low and taunting that makes the other warrior narrow his eyes at him.

On the shore, there are many different types of aliens going about their days, so focused on pulling in fishing nets and bargaining at the small market that they pay no attention to us.

I wanted a distraction, and I'm sure getting it here. I glance at Vivian, and her gaze is darting around like she doesn't know where to look first. I laugh.

"This place is crazy," I murmur as the warriors surround us.

"It's the closest thing to actual civilization I've seen since we got here. I'm a fan. Let's go explore."

She links her arm through mine, and we walk up the long dock. The Braxians surround us as we make our way down a narrow, cobbled street. The buildings are close together, and I glance up at where a blue alien is hanging laundry on a balcony. At every intersection, vendors have set up carts of food and tables holding jewelry, weapons, and clothes.

We turn to the right, and Tagiz points at the huge black castle. It's situated downhill, which is the only reason we couldn't see it from the dock. I wonder if this is a strategic move.

"How the hell are we going to get in there?" I murmur as we walk down the hill.

Duvix shrugs. "We sent a messenger ahead, asking for a meeting with Arix. The king," he says as I frown. "We haven't yet heard back, but he is aware that we are coming."

This does appear to be the case, as the guards leading to the castle allow us to pass each time that Hewex steps forward and murmurs to them.

"Am I the only one starting to get nervous?"

Vivian shakes her head. "I don't know what I was expecting, but it wasn't this."

The guards are dressed in spiffy black uniforms with gold buttons. They're armed with swords, and they stand at attention as we walk closer to the castle.

We cross a wooden bridge, and I take a moment to peer over the side, into the river below. People are traveling down the river in small, canoe-like contraptions, and a few of them glance up at us curiously.

Finally, we arrive at the castle entrance, waiting at the huge black doors, which are flung open.

Guards are standing at attention on each side, but they've obviously gotten the memo because they let us enter.

I gape at the walls, which must be a hundred feet high. The rock is a deep black, with veins of silver running through it, making the walls gleam. In front of us, a huge staircase is made out of what looks like white marble, the banister gleaming silver.

Vivian holds my arm tighter. "It doesn't even feel like we're on Agron anymore."

A guard approaches us. "You have been given an audience with the king," he says.

Jozet steps forward. He insists on walking first, with Duvix bringing up the rear, sandwiching us between them. Vivian and I likely look like tourists at Disney World, our heads turning from side to side as we follow the guard to the left and into a huge throne room.

It's lighter in here, with huge windows on either side allowing the sun to enter.

A long silver carpet leads from our feet to the throne. On either side, aliens of all kinds are sitting on plush sofas and chairs, talking amongst themselves. They go silent as we walk between them, toward the throne.

It's a deep jet black, gleaming like polished obsidian. An immense behemoth of a Braxian is currently lounging on it, a cup in one of his paddle-sized hands.

"Whoa," Vivian murmurs next to me. The giant Braxian's gaze lifts to me before flicking to Vivian's face, where it stays.

"Hello, lovely," he purrs, and for the first time, I see her blush.

She looks as surprised at the color of her cheeks as I am, shooting me a wide-eyed look. She recovers quickly, stepping closer. "Hello yourself."

His eyes—such a dark blue they're almost black—turn feral.

He gets to his feet, and I suck in a breath. Dragix is a big guy—taller and more built than any human man I've ever seen. But while he's lean, his movements a kind of rolling prowl, this tribe king is pure bulky muscle.

"You look like you've been bench-pressing that throne," Vivian says.

A Braxian sitting close to the throne leers at her. "You look like you're ready for a good, hard—"

Jozet steps forward and cuffs the guy around the head. The Braxian immediately jumps to his feet with a growl, while Vivian stares down at her feet, her cheeks flushing.

Arix retakes his throne, and the entire clearing goes deathly silent. He points to the loudmouth and then to the door behind us. The guy looks shocked but doesn't dare argue. Instead, he turns and shoves past Jozet, stalking out.

I clear my throat, and Arix glances at me. The remaining courtiers remain silent, obviously deciding that now is not a good time to piss him off.

"We have heard of the strange, tiny females who have mated with our barbarian cousins," Arix says. His eyes flick to Vivian's empty wrists and then return to me.

I almost laugh. If he thinks Rakiz and Dexar are barbarians, what would he think of Khax?

I don't know what to say to that.

Vivian clears her throat. "The Braxians have so far been most generous with their help."

"Is that right, lovely? And I'm guessing you're here to ask for some of that *generosity* for yourself."

He makes it sound incredibly dirty, but Vivian has regained her composure, and she simply raises one perfectly plucked eyebrow.

"You're right," she says. "We are currently looking for allies."

She explains our situation to the tribe king, who listens intently. He glances at me occasionally, but for the most part, his eyes stay steadily on her face, even after she falls silent.

I open my mouth and then clamp it shut as he flicks me a look.

All righty then.

Arix angles his head. "Why did Rakiz not come here himself?"

"He thought you would prefer to see why we need your help. As you mentioned, we are much smaller than Braxian females. If the aliens who are coming for us manage to take us with them..." She bites her lip and visibly shivers.

The woman deserves an Emmy for this performance.

The king's eyes soften minutely, and he stares at Vivian for a long moment, considering it.

"We have never worked with the barbaric tribes on the other side of the water before," he finally says. "There are reasons for that."

"There's a first time for everything," I say, and Arix gives me an unfriendly look. "Plus, if these guys are landing on Agron looking for us, who's to say they won't decide to take Braxian females with them as well? This entire planet is at risk."

Murmurs sound at that, and I glance at the courtiers. One of the Braxian women has turned pale, and a warrior—obviously her mate—pulls her into his arms, shooting me a look.

Arix ignores that, returning his attention to Vivian.

"We will think on it," he says. Then he stands, walking down the stairs that lead to his throne.

His voice is low, intimate as he gazes at Vivian. "If you are frightened, you may come here, pretty female. My guards will protect you with their lives."

Her eyes widen slightly at that. "Thank you for the offer," she says carefully. "But I will stay with the other human women. A threat to them is a threat to me."

He gives her a faint smile. "You are welcome if you change your mind." He glances at me. "You both are."

I nod, and we turn to leave, obviously dismissed. Nice of him to extend the offer to me, if only to attempt to entice Vivian to come to him for safety.

The Braxian warriors are silent as we walk back to the boat.

I lean close to Vivian. "What was that all about with you and Arix?"

She wrinkles her pert nose. "I have no idea. Let's hope he helps though. If those aliens are really coming back..."

"Yeah."

We'll need all the help we can get.

***

Charlie

Vivian and I are both exhausted when we finally get back to camp. She goes straight to her kradi, and I head back to Rakiz and Nevada's tashiv, finding them eating dinner.

"Hey, girl," Nevada says. "Are you hungry?"

"Starving."

Nevada turns to a woman who is currently carrying in a

platter of meat. "Arana, would you mind bringing an extra plate for Charlie?"

The Braxian woman smiles at me. "Of course."

I take a seat and attempt to ignore the intimate smile Nevada gives Rakiz as he strokes a hand down her hair. Why is it that it's so much harder to see happy couples when you're dealing with your own heartbreak?

"So how did it go?" Nevada asks.

I fill them in on what Arix said, and Nevada gets up to pace. Her shirt moves up, and I burst out laughing.

She turns to me. "What?"

I point, and she stares down with a rueful grin. Her leather pants, usually tied tight, are currently barely staying put. The strings that hold them around her waist are obviously straining with the effort, and they look close to snapping as she moves.

She grins. "Yeah, I've officially popped. I'm going to need some new pants." She glances at Rakiz, and the joy in his eyes is so fierce that I look away, giving them their moment.

Nevada turns back to me. "So he was interested in Vivian, huh?"

I smile at the reminder. "Enough that he offered her safety if she stayed with him."

"Wow."

I can see the wheels turning in Nevada's head as she glances back at Rakiz, and he stretches out his legs, raising one eyebrow.

"There's got to be some way we can use this," Nevada murmurs, and we all look up at a knock on the door.

One of the guards leans in, speaking directly to Rakiz. "Visitors. They insist you will want to speak to them."

Rakiz gets to his feet. "Show them in."

My mouth drops open as Khax strolls in. He glances

around the tashiv, his expression impressed, and nods at Rakiz before giving me a smile. It transforms his face, making him suddenly handsome, and I blink at him.

"You're going to help us?" I blurt out, and he nods again, turning his attention to Rakiz.

"After such pretty words from your alien females, and such an impressive gift, we decided to help. A threat to your females is a threat to all our females if these invaders are truly as dishonorable as you say."

I nod. "They are. If they conquer Agron, they could take as many women as they like."

Khax angles his head at that, and Rakiz steps forward.

"We have much to discuss."

Khax flashes his teeth. "I almost forgot. Since you brought a gift for my tribe, I brought one for yours." He turns to one of his warriors, who is standing guard by the door. He nods at him, and the warrior turns, returning moments later.

Rakiz growls, thrusting Nevada behind him as Khax's warrior drags one of the purple aliens forward.

I'm instantly shaking, barely tamping down the urge to bolt. One glance at Nevada's face tells me she's feeling the same way. But Khax's warrior has a steady grip on the alien, and he's unarmed.

"Their people are called the Dokhalls," Khax says. "We have not yet asked him for more information. We thought you would like to be present for that pleasure."

Rakiz nods, his eyes hard. Then he turns to Nevada.

"You don't need to be here for this," he murmurs.

She's pale, but her chin sticks out slightly as she glowers at the Dokhall. "I'll stay."

Rakiz glances at me, and I shake my head. "I'm peacing out." I turn to Khax. "Thank you for coming."

He nods, and I head for the door. From the fear on the Dokhall's pale-purple face, he knows exactly what's about to happen to him.

Torture.

The most savage part of me is glad. *That* Charlie wants to sit and watch as the Dokhall screams.

But I have enough nightmares without adding to them. I've done my part for today.

Instead, I wander through the camp until I find Alexis.

"Those new arrivals are getting straight to work," she says as soon as she sees me. "Want to come see?"

I'm more than a little curious, and I nod, trailing after her as she leaves the camp. Three of Dexar's guards are following us, but Alexis doesn't appear to notice as we walk through the grassy meadow until we reach the edge of the forest.

"Where are we?"

Alexis points straight ahead. "If we traveled for a few hours, we'd be in the Seinex Forest. This is a much smaller forest in comparison, but according to our scouts, those purple aliens have made themselves at home in the Seinex."

I nod. "They're called Dokhalls, by the way. Rakiz is currently torturing one of them for information."

Alexis nods. "Awesome."

I stare at her, and she rolls her eyes. "Oh, come on, Charlie. They bought us like we were pigs in a market. Look what they did to Zoey! I'm not going to feel bad about making them pay for that."

"I get it," I say. "It's just...torture freaks me out. We're meant to be better than them."

"I know. But think about what they'd do to us. If they find out what the Dokhalls are planning, it could save lives. Our lives."

"Yeah. I just wish we didn't have to do it, you know. I wish they would just fuck off."

"On that we can agree," Alexis says. We turn a corner, and I gape at the ten or fifteen shirtless Braxian warriors currently working together to dig a huge hole. A hole so long and wide that I can't quite understand what it could be for.

Ivy and Vrex are watching the Braxians, both of them looking pleased.

"Yum," Alexis murmurs, her eyes on the warriors. I give her a look. "What? I'm mated, not dead."

I grin, and we stroll up to the warriors. One of them glances at us, and I raise my eyebrow.

"What's that going to be?"

"Trap."

I eye the Braxian who seems to be the leader of this little gang, and he flashes his white teeth at me as he grins.

He explains how the trap will work, and I study the surrounding area, impressed.

"But how will you get them here?"

"Bait."

"And one of us will need to play bait."

He nods, and the warrior next to him laughs. "Fast bait. Real fast."

I think about the other women. Most of them have mates, and from what I've seen so far, they're likely to forbid them from this kind of thing. Zoey still gets winded if she walks too fast, so she's out. Vivian...I misjudged Vivian when I first got here, but I can't imagine her hauling ass through the forest with a bunch of aliens on her heels.

"I'll do it."

Ivy steps up behind us, examining the trap. "It's going to be dangerous as hell," she says. "Are you sure?"

"I'm fast and sneaky. I'm our best shot. But I'm going to have to practice."

She shivers beside me, and Alexis moves closer, wrapping her arm around my shoulders.

"I wish none of us had to do any of this stuff," she murmurs. "I wish they'd just leave us alone."

I sigh. "Me too."

CHAPTER SEVENTEEN

D ragix

I fly over the forest, looking for the purple invaders. Each time I find one, I swoop down, killing it with flame. However, after several days of this, they have gotten wiser to the threat I present. Now they have hidden themselves, likely in a cave or underground.

I have not been able to locate their ship.

I turn and fly toward my mountain. I am...lost without my little two-leg. Is this to be my life? Long days of boredom, of fighting not to go to Charlie, of wondering if she is safe?

Is this what eternity feels like?

Charlie will die. Her life span is the blink of an eye compared to mine. And I will go on, and on, and on without her.

The thought makes me roar, and the animals below me scatter.

All I can see is Charlie's beautiful smile. Her curly hair,

smooth pale skin, and blue eyes. All I can hear is her laugh. The strangled gasp she would make as I entered her.

What good is eternity if I spend it alone? If Charlie lives without me?

I have been wrong.

My family wouldn't want me to spend my life alone, a shadow of myself. In my mind, I can see my mother, dancing around our lair with my father. Flying over our territory with him, their wings almost touching. Gazing indulgently at my sister and me as we raced through our home.

I land in the small clearing where my family is buried. I shift, falling to my knees as I stare at their graves.

I thought my people would want me to survive above anything else. But Maez's words ring true.

"You got to live. It's up to you what you do with that precious gift, but from the stories I've heard about your mother, she wouldn't want you to waste it. She'd want you to make the most of the years you have."

I have been so focused on my rage, so determined to stay alive, that I forgot what life is meant to be about.

Eternity spent flying over these lands, always alone, never seeing my little two-leg again?

I would rather have a short life span with Charlie than centuries more of loneliness.

I would rather have one day with her than a hundred years knowing that she has gone to the great beyond without me.

Why did it take me so long to truly understand?

As if the realization was all I needed, I can suddenly *feel* Charlie. I gasp, understanding.

Mated. My mate is alone and in danger. I did this.

Her terror makes my hands shake, and I shift back instantly, propelling myself into the sky with a roar.

How could I have been so stupid? How could I have been so...arrogant?

I can hear the sounds of war long before I get close to the Braxian camp. I fly low, scouting the forest, and then curse as a bright light flashes, shooting past my wing.

I dodge, glancing down as the purple two-legs fire at me from their ship.

I wouldn't have noticed the ship if they had not fired. They've managed to camouflage it, layering branches and leaves on top of it until it's almost impossible to spot from above.

I roar, and the purple invaders scatter. Some of them must be on the ship as it fires at me, but I'm too fast, evading them with a simple maneuver that allows me to get close enough to spit fire at them.

They die, screaming, and I growl in satisfaction. I set the surrounding forest on fire and land behind the ship. No bright lights are firing from the back of the ship, and I let out a pleased rumble as purple two-legs pour from the ship, long sticks in their hands. They attempt to surround me, but unlike their ship, their weapons don't fire the same bright, burning light.

But I am too fast for them. One by one, they attempt to dart forward and touch me with their sticks. And one by one, they die.

I take a deep breath, ready to burn the ship until it is nothing but molten metal. If there are still purple two-legs inside, they are quiet, likely hiding.

"Dragix?"

I spin and find the flame-haired female staring at me. *Ivy,* I remember. Charlie likes her. Charlie likes all the human females. Her Braxian mate is next to her, and I ignore him, once again readying myself to destroy the ship and prevent the purple two-legs from taking the human females off this planet.

That's when I hear it.

I angle my head, and Ivy stares at me.

Her eyes narrow at whatever she sees. "What is it?"

"I hear females. Screaming."

"Holy shit," she says. "You can talk in my head?"

Her warrior steps closer and wraps an arm around her waist, obviously displeased at whatever intimacy he thinks this provides.

"There may still be purple two-legs inside."

She relays this information to the Braxian.

He draws his sword. "I will go first."

She frowns at this but doesn't argue. She's holding her own sword, but obviously she knows better than to think a male on this planet would allow a female to walk into danger ahead of him.

I take a deep breath, putting out the flames surrounding us. Then I shift forms, and Ivy takes a step back.

"Hoo boy," she murmurs. "I forgot you could do that."

"Where is Charlie?"

She gives me a look. "Why do you care? You abandoned her, remember?"

I snarl, and the Braxian warrior narrows his eyes at us.

"Perhaps we could discuss this later," he growls.

I bare my teeth as I stalk past him, moving up the cool metal ramp that leads into the ship. A purple two-leg immediately lunges at me, and I bat his stick aside, hitting him in the face. He crumbles, falling to the ground.

That felt good. There was something oddly satisfying about the thud of my fist against an enemy. Perhaps this wingless form is not as useless as I had imagined it to be.

There are two more two-legs hiding in the front of the

ship. The Braxian stalks past me and ends them, and then we turn toward the screams.

"Help! Please, someone help us!"

Ivy rushes forward, but the Braxian grabs her arm, thrusting her behind him. He sends her a warning look, and she rolls her eyes but allows it. The sight of her eye roll reminds me so much of Charlie that my whole body aches for her.

The Braxian prowls forward, and my eyes water at the stench.

"Oh my God," Ivy says.

Human females. At least thirty of them, all in a cage. Many of them are crying, while others are screaming. One of them stares at me, her gaze drops below my waist, and she begins softly sobbing.

"We're not going to hurt you," Ivy says.

"Then get us out of here," one of the females snaps.

I examine the cage, ignoring the screams of the females as I approach. The cage has some kind of mechanism, and I survey the latch.

Ivy steps forward. "How did they get it open?"

"That panel right there," one of the females says, wiping tears off her cheeks. "I think they used their palm prints."

The Braxian stalks away before returning with a purple hand, blood dripping from the wrist.

Several of the females gag, but most of them cheer as he holds the hand to the square panel and the cage door slowly opens.

Ivy turns to me. "We need to make sure that everyone is off this ship before we destroy it."

The female who ordered us to open the cage steps forward, pushing tangled white-blonde hair away from her face.

"Are you kidding?" she snaps. "This is our ride out of here."

Ivy stares at her. "There are hundreds of these purple bastards currently marching on one of our camps. If that camp falls, all of us could end up back on this ship and taken God knows where."

Another female steps forward, wrapping her arms around herself as if she's cold.

"There're not hundreds of them," she says. "They must have close to a thousand. They knew they were coming here to fight."

Ivy curses, and the white-blonde female sighs.

"Can't we wait? If you have people willing to fight, can't they come guard this ship? If it looks like they're going to be killed, we can always destroy it then."

Ivy looks unhappy at this, and the first female narrows her eyes at her.

"We're not staying on this planet," she announces. "We're using this ship to get out of here."

Enough of this. I turn to Ivy. "Where is Charlie?"

She bites her lip, and something like dread sinks to the bottom of my stomach.

"She volunteered," she says softly, and I stare at her.

"*Where* is my *mate?*"

"The Dokhalls are attacking. We were sent to scout for their ship. Charlie...Charlie is playing bait. She's leading them toward a trap so we can attempt to cull their numbers."

Horror slams into me. "Bait?"

The other females are murmuring amongst themselves, some of them pushing past us to leave the ship in search of fresh air.

"You left her," Ivy snaps. "She's doing what she felt was right."

I don't stay to hear more. I stalk out of the ship and shift into my winged form, ignoring the females' gasps.

Then I take to the air and begin the search for my mate.

Charlie

The tribe kings have been planning for this battle for days.

At least that's what I tell myself as I watch the Dokhalls march on us.

I asked Nevada why they bothered. Why they would work so hard and risk so many lives for a few human women.

She just snorted, her face pale as we stood on a hill near the small forest close to Rakiz's camp. "They're not the decision makers. Someone sitting in a cushy office on their home planet will have given the order. These guys? These guys are just meat."

Now we're all silent as one of the Dokhalls leaves the front lines, moving toward us. He gets close enough that I can see every feature of his pale-purple face. Every horn curving up from his head.

"Last chance," he calls. "Give us the females and we will leave."

Dexar simply stares at him. Then he raises his arm and slashes it down.

The air becomes full of arrows along with the tresla pods that work almost like bombs. The Dokhalls didn't see them coming, likely assuming that the Braxians were only armed with swords.

The Dokhalls begin to go down, but for every purple creature who falls, another is there to replace them.

There are so many of them. And the weapons they carry, the ones that look like sticks? As soon as the Dokhalls charge at the Braxians, the Braxians begin to fall.

They don't even need to touch them with the pointed end of their weapons. They just need to be within a few feet of our warriors, and a blue light sparks from their weapons, dropping the Braxians like flies.

We may have thousands more Braxians on our side, but for every Dokhall we kill, several more Braxians go down.

Beside me, Nevada lets another arrow loose from her crossbow. Beside her, Beth is doing the same, while Ivy has gone with Vrex to hunt for the Dokhalls' ship.

Alexis has ordered the warriors to collect any of the Dokhalls' weapons they can find, and she's currently crouched behind our hill, attempting to figure out how one of them works. If we can turn their weapons against them, we'll have a better shot at winning this battle.

Zoey and Ellie are in the healers' kradi, taking care of the wounded, and Vivian...

Vivian is currently lighting tresla pods on fire and hauling them at the Dokhalls, a fierce grin on her face.

I take a moment to look at the women with me. To take a mental picture. To say goodbye.

Nevada meets my eyes, and I can't hear her over the sounds of the battle, but I read her lips.

"You got this," she tells me.

I give her a shaky smile, and then I get to my feet.

I move to the side, a crossbow in my hand. I'm useless with it, but I attempt to hit the Dokhalls as I position myself close to the edge of the forest.

I glance at Rakiz, who's sitting on his mishua. As soon as

the Dokhalls' front line falls, our best warriors will be headed straight for the center of the battle.

He turns his head and meets my eyes for one long moment. He argued against this. It seems to be against Braxian code to allow women to be in danger.

But after a whispered fight with Nevada, he finally gave in. Rakiz says something to the warriors surrounding him, and their mishua move further from me. They make it look like a simple break in their defenses as a group of the Dokhalls attack.

Can't make it obvious.

I'm so scared that I'm trembling, my mouth dry as the last mishua moves, and I make myself widen my eyes as if wondering what the hell happened to my protection.

It seems like the Dokhalls' entire left flank breaks away. They're practically falling over each other to be the one to bring me back to their ship. I wonder if they have some reward system. Maybe each of us human women is worth a certain amount of points.

I whip my head from side to side, but as planned, Rakiz is long gone and Terex has already moved closer to the front lines. He's roaring as if he's in a killing rage, unable to remember that he's meant to defend me.

The Dokhalls are getting closer. By now, they'll see exactly which way I'll be running.

So I turn and sprint into the forest as if I've lost all self-control. As if I'm so terrified and stupid that I leave the protection of the Braxians behind.

The Dokhalls don't want to kill me. So if this plan succeeds, I will have taken fifty or more enemies from the front lines, removing them as threats to the Braxians.

And increasing all our chances of surviving.

I've run this route a hundred times. The Braxians helped

me dig up anything I could trip on before covering up the evidence so it wouldn't be obvious that I'm leading the Dokhalls down a well-traveled path.

But I didn't expect them to be so fucking fast.

I'm more out of shape than I'd like. In Houston, I spent some of my precious tip money on a pass for the gym—not to work out, but so I could use the shower each day. I preferred running outside, but when it got too hot, I occasionally hit the treadmill. I hate running, but the thought of Ben chasing me was enough to motivate me to get my four miles in each morning.

This isn't close to four miles, but it needs to be taken as a sprint. And it can't look like I'm leading them anywhere. I turn right, grabbing the long white branch of the tree I marked earlier and using it for leverage as I swing around the corner.

I need them to see where I'm going.

That's not a problem, though, because they're gaining on me, those horrible sticks in their hands. They clutch them like spears, and I lower my head, pumping my legs faster.

Crashing sounds are coming from the trees to my right. They've split up, and they're trying to cut me off.

Shit.

It's okay, Charlie. You planned for this. Keep your eye on the ball.

I'm more winded than I usually am at this point in the run, terror clutching at my throat, making it harder to breathe. But the adrenaline keeps me throwing one foot in front of the other, keeps my arms pumping as I head down the final stretch.

Both groups are getting close. When I mentioned this possibility to the Braxians who set up this trap, they simply tilted their heads, stared into the forest, and told me they'd take care of it.

I really hope they took care of it.

The rope is around the next turn, and I can see it in my mind's eye, dangling in front of me. I was never good at gym, but I'm going to have to scramble up that rope like a spider monkey, and I'm going to have to do it before the aliens chasing me see me.

If this doesn't work, I'm worse than dead.

It's Dragix's face that flashes in front of my eyes as I round the final corner and lunge for the rope. Dragix's eyes that urge me on as I take three huge steps and jump for it, my momentum making it swing wildly as I scale it.

I reach for the branch of the tree and haul myself onto it, immediately pulling the rope up after me. My breath is coming in wild sobs, and I slam my hand over my mouth, crouching in my branch as I hear the Dokhalls yelling.

But someone else is calling me, his voice frantic in my head.

"Charlie? Charlie!"

Dragix? Is he...here?

I block him out as the Dokhalls round the corner. Some of them are furious, eyes hard, snarling as they tear down the path. Others seem to be having fun, savage grins on their faces as they yell insults down the trail at where they think I'm still running.

I slam my eyes shut, terrified that they'll feel my eyes on them, that they'll look up and see me in this tree.

They don't.

The stream past my tree, and for a second, I think the trap hasn't worked. I'm suddenly sure that they'll keep running, realize I'm not up ahead, and circle back to find me.

Just when I'm frantically attempting to figure out another plan, the air fills with screams.

I peek through my hands as I turn my head and look down at the trap.

The ground has given way, just like it was supposed to.

Ten feet below, the purple bastards who thought they could steal me off this planet are impaled on sharpened sticks, rocks, and even the occasional knife.

They're not going anywhere until they can dig themselves out. And a group of Braxians will be arriving soon to finish this job.

I stay put for a long moment, terrified that the group that was trying to cut me off might be on its way.

But they don't break through the trees, even as their friends scream for help.

I climb through the branches of the tree to the other side and let down another rope. I swing down, attempting to block out the sounds of the dying aliens.

They could have left us in peace. But they came to this planet because they consider us property.

This is war.

CHAPTER EIGHTEEN

D ragix

I scan the battle below, desperately searching for Charlie. I blow out a stream of fire, aiming at the Dokhalls crowding too close to the Braxians on the right flank.

They turn to ash.

Cheers sound, the Braxians waving their swords in the air. I ignore them, my heart pounding in my chest.

I see both Braxian tribe queens. I see the white-haired two-leg who Charlie called Vivian gleefully throwing small pods at the Dokhalls and smiling when they explode.

But I don't see Charlie.

"Little two-leg, where are you?"

I call her again and again, flying further from the battle.

"I'm here, Dragix."

Relief makes me shudder, and my wings tremble as I glance down, finding Charlie beaming up at me as she sprints out of the trees.

I land, snatching her to me and running the top of one claw gently down her face as I check for damage.

"You came," she says, and I nod, picking her up and placing her on my back.

"I couldn't leave you to fight without me. Never again will you be without me."

Charlie lets out a sound that sounds like a cross between a laugh and a sob. And then I turn my head, finding a group of purple two-legs creeping closer, pointed weapons in their hands.

I snarl at them, spit fire, and take Charlie to the sky.

"Oh God," she says. "Dragix...we're losing this battle."

She's right. I lean down and blow fire through the center of the Dokhalls. But it's not enough to turn them to ash. Not anymore.

Charlie's legs tense around me as the Dokhalls scream, attempting to put out the flames that ravage their bodies.

"What's going on, Dragix?"

"I only have so much flame, little two-leg. I have been hunting the purple invaders already today and have not eaten enough to replenish my fire."

"Oh shit."

I watch the purple two-legs. They scream and run in circles, attempting to put out the flames engulfing them. It provides a good distraction as the invaders near them move away, scared of the flames.

But it's not enough.

The Braxians are slowly retreating, likely hoping to get behind the camp walls. There are thousands of Braxians, but their swords are no match for the Dokhall weapons, which spit blue light.

So many of them have fallen that they are slumped on each other, the ground a sea of bodies.

Alexis is handing the Braxians the Dokhall weapons that she has obviously ordered to be collected. From the way she's holding them and screaming at the Braxians, she's teaching them how to use them.

"Dragix, she needs more weapons. Can we help?"

I swoop down, plucking the long sticks from fallen Dokhalls, and Alexis lets out a cheer as we dump them at her feet.

But it's too late. The Braxians' right flank has fallen, giving the Dokhalls a clear path to the human females.

Rakiz turns his head, roaring at Nevada to *move,* and she nods, her face pale as she glances around her.

But she is now surrounded.

"Dragix!" Charlie is screaming, pointing at Nevada.

One of the purple two-legs has obviously decided against taking the human females back to his ship. He has lost his weapon, but he picks up a sword, a savage grin on his face. Revenge. It's clear that he wants vengeance for his fallen friends.

He's holding Nevada's sword.

She's clutching a crossbow, and she aims it at him. He dodges left as she shoots, missing his chest as the bolt hits his arm.

Charlie lets out a dry sob as I arrow toward Nevada, planning to snatch her from the ground.

Beth is suddenly there, a crossbow in her hand as she aims at the Dokhall. But Vivian gets to Nevada first, her mouth grim, her face set in determination as she steps in front of Nevada, pushing her to the ground.

The Dokhall slides his sword into her chest.

Nevada, Beth, and Charlie are screaming as I reach the Dokhall, my claws slashing. His head rolls to the ground, but it may be too late for the two-leg female.

"Oh God, oh God," Charlie is crying as she jumps off my back and falls to her knees beside Nevada.

Nevada is screaming. "Why, Vivian? Why would you do that?"

The female's lips are bloody, a bad sign. "You're pregnant," she says with a weak smile, and Nevada sobs, clutching Vivian to her as she rocks.

Beth screams for a healer, and one of them rushes forward from behind the hill.

"I will attempt to heal her." I glance down at the bleeding female. I want to tell Charlie that it is too late, that Vivian is losing too much blood. But I must at least try.

Rakiz is suddenly next to Nevada, his face white as he stares down at Vivian.

"She saved my life," Nevada tells him, and he pulls her into his arms, his eyes closing for a moment in relief. His expression is tormented as he stares down at the bleeding female—the female under his protection.

I lean down and examine the wound. Then I get to work, pushing my saliva deep into the female's chest.

"What the hell is he doing?" Beth demands.

"Healing her," Charlie says. "Just like he healed me."

"Holy shit," Nevada says. Then her voice goes low. "We're losing, aren't we?"

Rakiz's tone is gentle. "Yes, karja."

Rakiz leans close to me as I lick between the female's ribs.

"I need you to take the females away from here," he murmurs.

Nevada and Beth are instantly protesting, both of them covered in Vivian's blood as the female barely clings to life. Charlie just looks at me and shakes her head.

I ignore that and nod at Rakiz. Then I move back from

Vivian. *"I have done all I can, but I am not a god. She has lost a lot of blood."*

The healer takes over, dripping some kind of concoction into Vivian's mouth, and then we all turn as a loud horn sounds from the battlefield.

Charlie scrambles to her feet, and I pull her onto my back where she can see.

The Dokhalls are falling.

Falling to an army that marches toward us, carrying gleaming black shields that protect them from the blue lights of the Dokhalls' weapons.

"Oh my God," Charlie says. "It's Arix. He actually came."

She's pointing to a Braxian on the front lines. He's riding a scaled beast, and a black crown gleams on his head.

He glances across the battlefield and salutes us with his sword as Charlie lets out a whoop of relief.

"Eat, Dragix. I need you to eat."

"I don't want to leave you."

"With Arix's forces and your fire, we can kill them. Please, Dragix, I'll be fine."

I help her off my back and turn to Rakiz. He nods, and I lean down, running my snout against Charlie's head.

"Very well."

I don't go far. I take to the skies and then swoop down, plucking Dokhalls from their lines. The most cowardly turn and run, heading for the cover of trees as the Dokhalls are suddenly caught between Arix's warriors at their backs and the remaining Braxians at their fronts.

The Dokhalls taste almost as bitter as the Voildi, but I crunch down anyway. I instantly have more energy, and I immediately turn it to flame, burning my way through the Dokhalls.

But I get too close.

And I have forgotten.

Forgotten that I am still mortal now. That I have not spent enough time in this form to undo the damage that has been done.

Their weapons burn, hotter than any flame, as they hit my wings. I roar, and Charlie's panicked scream pierces through the sound of the battle.

I go down, crushing them as I fall. They're savage, advancing on me in a horde, weapons pointed toward me.

I may be grounded, but I'm not helpless. My wings burn, coldness spreading up them and into my back. It's as if I've been poisoned.

Whatever makes their weapons spit blue light is the antithesis of my flames.

The purple two-legs soon stop advancing, choosing instead to wait, just out of reach of my flames.

"Dragix!"

I turn my head, roaring at the sight of Charlie sprinting toward me.

"What are you doing? Get back behind the hill."

She ignores that, a sword in her hand, and I tremble at the sight of her running straight into danger.

Then the purple two-legs are dying, attempting to flee as they're attacked from all sides. Several of them back up, coming within my range, and I spit flames at them, watching in satisfaction as they have to run toward the other purple two-legs who are still attempting to escape from Arix and his warriors.

It's suddenly quiet.

The remaining purple two-legs have either fled or have been cut down, the battlefield scattered with their weapons.

My eyes slide closed as my legs are no longer able to hold my weight.

The battle is over.

Charlie

I'm screaming wordlessly as I slump to my knees next to Dragix. His bright gold eyes are closed, but he seems to rouse at my howling, cracking them open slightly, although they're glassy and unfocused.

"Shift back," I demand, and he closes his eyes again. "Damn you, Dragix, shift back so we can help you!"

He lets out a long, breathy sigh, but he complies.

It takes a long time.

Gold sparks are rising around us, and I sob as his body seems to shift inch by inch. His snout gets smaller, his teeth disappearing, and I have to close my eyes briefly at the gruesome sight.

The fact that his shift is taking so long is not a good sign.

Distantly, I'm aware that we're surrounded. Arix is standing in front of us, staring down at Dragix, his sword in his hand as if he's contemplating taking his head while he's vulnerable. I bare my teeth at him, and the ghost of a smile crosses his face as he meets my eyes.

"Why isn't he healing?" I ask, my voice high and thready. "Dragix, why aren't you healing?"

Moni is suddenly next to me, her expression mournful.

"Don't look at him like that," I snap. "He's going to be fine. Dragix, open your eyes."

He does. His expression is tender as he attempts to raise his hand to my face. His arm falls, and I catch his hand in mine, bringing it to my cheek.

"Why aren't you healing?" My tears are dripping down his hand, and his eyes are full of sorrow.

"I am...no longer immortal, my little two-leg."

I stare at him. "What?"

"I spent too much time in my wingless form. It is the way of my people."

"No. Why would you do this? Why come back here if you can die?"

"Worth it," he tells me, his voice weak. "Worth it to see you, to hear your voice."

I lean over, pressing kisses to his face as my tears slide onto his skin. "Please, Dragix. Please don't leave me."

This is all my fault. I knew he hadn't eaten enough. Knew he was weak. And I told him to attack the Dokhalls.

His gaze is steady on my face. "I love you, Charlie. You shook me awake when I was sleeping. You brought me back to life. I tried to go back to the way I was before. To living only in my winged form. But all I could think of was you. Your eyes, your smile, the way you fought me at every turn and then made me want things I had never wanted before."

I let out a sob. "So stay. Stay with me. We can have a future together, Dragix. I'll stay here on Agron with you. We'll go back to our mountain and shut out the world."

His smile is soft, indulgent, and sad as his eyes slide closed.

I howl, weeping against him. This can't be the end. He can't tell me all that and then leave me here alone. Without him.

"Oh my God," Vivian says, and I glance up, tears hot on my face. She's clutched in Jozet's arms. Her pale-blue dress is covered in so much blood that it looks brown, and Arix steps forward, his lips thinning at the sight of her.

"What happened?" he snaps.

"I was...dying. Dragix healed me. Put me down," Vivian says, and Jozet complies, setting her on the ground next to me. "I'm so sorry, Charlie."

"He's not dead," I snap. "Don't say it like that."

Ellie and Zoey are suddenly here too, and next to them, Ivy stands, a large group of human women behind her, murmuring quietly amongst themselves. I can't even bring myself to be curious. To care.

Nevada steps close and sits down on my other side, a silent support.

I can't lose him. Not my fierce, gentle dragon.

I should never have made him bring me back here.

"We were happy," I murmur. "We were happy on his mountain."

Nevada wraps her arm around me, and Vivian lets out a choked sob next to me.

Arix steps closer at the sound, ignoring my hiss. "I may be able to help," he says.

My stomach flutters as I stare at him. "Please. Please."

He ignores that, turning his attention to Vivian.

"You wish for him to live?"

"God, yes."

He gestures, and a Braxian woman steps forward, a small wooden container in her hand.

"What is it?" I ask as she kneels next to Dragix, opening the container.

Arix's eyes are on Vivian's face as he replies, "Cava berries. They are our most precious resource. They allow healing when it would seem that there is no hope."

More tears slip down my face at his words. Please, please let them work. Please.

The healer squeezes the bright-blue berries against Dragix's lips, and I reach forward, helping her open his mouth. She places the berries inside, and we all watch as they stay in his mouth.

She gives me a sympathetic look. "He must swallow," she says.

I nod. He'll swallow these goddamned berries if I have to shove them down his throat.

"Dragix," I try. I switch to our mental pathway. I remember him telling me I was too loud, that I was shouting in his head.

And I scream at him. *"Dragix, you giant pain in my ass! You don't get to leave me, do you hear me? You made me fall in love with you, and it's not going to end like this. Wake up and swallow, damn it. Now!"*

Dragix takes a giant, shuddering breath. He doesn't open his eyes. He doesn't even reply.

But he swallows.

CHAPTER NINETEEN

D ragix

I can hear the low murmur of voices, and I frown. My eyes are too heavy to lift, but I can smell the sweet, fresh scent of my little two-leg. I can feel her soft hand stroking my cheek.

"Dragix?"

"I am unable to speak or open my eyes, Charlie. But I am here."

She lets out a choked sob and nestles closer to me, burying her face in my neck. I wish I could stroke her hair, could give her the slightest comfort, but I am paralyzed.

The thought sends a ripple of fear through my body, and that is enough to allow me to lift one finger.

I rest, exhausted from that slight motion.

"Where the hell did all those women come from?"

I recognize Nevada's voice. It's the flame-haired one—Ivy —who answers her.

"They were on the ship. Same story as us. They were

abducted by the Grivath and sold to the Dokhalls. It sounds like those poor women were on that ship for weeks. One of them said that the Dokhalls were ordered to come to Agron and search for us before they were allowed to return to their planet."

"That must have been hell," Ellie says. "It was bad enough for us, and we were only there for a few hours."

"Yeah," Ivy replies. "The healers want to check them over. Actually, I'll go find them now."

I manage to crack open my eyes. I'm in the healers' kradi, and the first person I see is Rakiz, who has Nevada in his lap as he clutches her to him, as if afraid to let go.

He grins at me, flashing white teeth. "Charlie," he murmurs, "it seems your dragon is awake."

Charlie jolts, lifting her head and grinning down at me. I raise my arm, and it shakes with the effort it costs me. But I manage to bury my hand in her soft hair and pull her head to mine so I can take her mouth.

She lets out a low laugh against my lips. *"Why am I not surprised that this is your first move after you were unconscious for hours?"*

I smile as she pulls her head back, staring down at me as if memorizing my face.

"What happened?" I ask.

"The Dokhalls scattered. Most of them are dead, but some of them got away. We won, Dragix. There's not enough of them to take us away. We even have their ship, although it was damaged when the Dokhalls returned to it and attempted to take it. Vrex and Ivy had a bunch of Braxians guarding it with them, but they managed to set it on fire."

"I am not sad to know that you can't leave me," I tease, and she gives me a look.

"I'm not leaving you," she says. "You scared the hell out of me, you know."

I nod, pulling her close again. She looks exhausted, the skin beneath her eyes dark and puffy and her face pale. But she has never been more beautiful to me.

"Rest, little two-leg. We will talk properly when we are alone."

She nods, snuggling closer to me, and I manage to turn my head. The healers are busy, moving from bed to bed as they help the wounded Braxians. In the bed next to mine, Vivian is somehow managing to sleep through the commotion.

The human females are sitting on small wooden stools, huddled around our beds. Rakiz gets to his feet, places Nevada back on his seat, and kisses her forehead.

"I must meet with Dexar," he says.

She nods, giving him a small smile.

"Rest," he says, and Nevada rolls her eyes but nods and then turns to Alexis.

"What's the deal with the ship?" she asks. "How badly damaged is it?"

"I've only had a quick look," Alexis says. "The good news is that this ship is in much better condition than the hunk of junk we landed here in. But the fuselage is cracked, and one of the thrusters was damaged."

All the females are silent.

Ivy steps inside. "Moni? The women are saying that they can wait. They don't want to take time and attention away from injured Braxians."

The healer smiles at her. "Thanks to the king from across the Colossal Water, we have enough healers to see to our wounded. He has brought healers with skills and abilities that we could not have imagined."

Ivy hesitates but finally nods, flicking her bright hair

over her shoulder as she turns, murmuring to someone outside.

Charlie moves her head from my shoulder to my chest, turning it so she can see what's going on. I stroke my hand down her back, more content than I could have imagined in this moment.

The white-haired female steps inside, her eyes immediately surveying the tent suspiciously. And then her eyes land on Vivian.

"Viv?" Her tone is incredulous, and she ignores everyone else in the kradi as she rushes to Vivian's side, sitting on her bed.

Vivian cracks open her eyes. She scowls, but then her eyes widen as she stares at the female. "Sarissa?"

They laugh, hugging and rocking and paying no attention to anyone else in the kradi. Charlie laughs at the sight, her small body shaking against mine, and I smile at the sound.

They're talking over each other, and my eyes slide closed as I listen to Vivian introduce the female to the others.

Cousins, she says, and I frown, reaching for my pathway with Charlie.

"What is this word?"

Charlie strokes her hand along my chest, and my body begins to respond. Someone has covered me with a blanket, but Charlie can obviously feel what is happening because her voice is amused.

"Sarissa is Vivian's mother or father's sibling's child."

I nod. I had these once. Ezra and I would race them through the forest, playing games that centered around attempting to hide our scents from one another.

Charlie seems to sense my sadness because she leans up

and places a gentle kiss on my lips. The females are talking, and Charlie pulls away.

"I'm Charlie," she says. "It's nice to meet you."

"You too. We owe you guys a thank-you for finding us. You especially, Ivy."

"No problem, really."

Nevada clears her throat. "We'll get you guys sorted with kradis and clothes and anything else you could need. I'm sorry you were taken, but you'll be safe here."

Sarissa angles her head. "I appreciate that. But while we'd love to enjoy your hospitality temporarily, we're hoping to fix the ship and leave."

Silence.

Alexis's voice is careful. "You know, there's no guarantee that it can even be fixed. As you've probably noticed, this isn't the most developed planet."

"I know. But we have to try. We made a deal when we were in that cage. We swore that if we could, we'd hunt down the bastards that took us and make them pay."

"I'm going too," Vivian says. "I have to," she continues over the other females' protests. "I love you guys, but I don't belong here. We all know that. And if I have a chance to make the Grivath pay while spending time with Sarissa? I'm going to do it."

I begin to drift off as the females debate the wisdom of this plan. Cool hands touch my brow, and I tense, but Charlie soothes me.

"It's just one of the healers," she says.

I nod and allow it. Then I force open my eyes at Arix's low voice.

He stands at the entrance of the kradi, his dark gaze examining everyone and everything before landing on Vivian.

"How are you feeling?" he murmurs, ignoring the silence in the kradi as everyone stares at him.

"Much better," Vivian says, a hint of color creeping up her cheeks. "Thank you."

I clear my throat and attempt to speak. "You have my deepest gratitude as well," I tell him, and he glances at me, nods, and then returns his attention to Vivian.

"I had thought I'd be in his debt," I say to Charlie, who has her eyes narrowed on Arix.

"Same. I don't trust him. He thought about killing you when you were dying, Dragix."

I raise my eyebrows at that. *"Interesting."*

"Interesting?" Charlie's tone is outraged, and I can't help but smile.

"I am the largest predator on this planet. The fact that he thought about killing me tells me that he is a wise ruler."

Charlie snorts at that.

Arix takes a step closer to Vivian's bed, and Sarissa glares at him as if he's a dangerous, poisonous creature.

"I couldn't help but overhear your plans to leave the planet," he says, gesturing toward the entrance to the kradi, where he must have been listening. "It is likely that you would find a solution to your problems in my city," he says softly. "We have many alchemists who tinker with metal and heat."

Vivian blinks at that. "One thing I've learned is that nothing in this universe is without a price. What's yours?"

He gives her a slow smile. "We can discuss that when you're feeling better," he says. "I would not be honorable if I entered negotiations with someone who was still recovering from blood loss."

Vivian's eyes flash at that, and Arix's smile widens.

"I will see you soon," he promises, and then, with a nod to me and a wink at Charlie, he strolls out of the kradi.

Rakiz enters next, his gaze going straight to Nevada. He narrows his eyes at her, and she throws up her hands.

"I'm going to go take a nap soon, I swear. Things were just getting way too interesting around here to leave."

The females laugh, and Rakiz steps closer to me. Dexar enters behind him, and I tense.

"I would like to sit up, little two-leg."

Charlie lifts her head and bites her lip. "Are you sure?"

I nod, and she moves off me, helping me sit. The kradi whirls around me, and I take a deep breath, finally focusing on Dexar and Rakiz.

"We would like to thank you for your help in the battle today," Dexar says formally, and Rakiz nods.

"I came here for Charlie," I say, and she elbows me gently in the ribs.

"Play nice."

I sigh. "You are welcome."

Rakiz steps closer. "We would also like to take this opportunity to formally apologize for our ancestors. By now, you know that it was not us that slaughtered your people. But we understand why you would hate us for it. In Braxian culture, there are few forms of payment and symbols of apology more powerful than a favor. Each of us would like to give you a favor that you may use for anything that it is in our power to give you. Except for our mates," he says quickly, and I snort.

I have my Charlie. Why would I be interested in their females?

"You do not have to accept," he says at my silence. "But know that we will forever be in your debt for the actions of our people. That our people will protect you from those who mean to kill you and take your scales. We are not long-lived like you. We may not remember your people, but for you, what you suffered must feel like it happened yesterday."

"It does."

Charlie is quiet next to me, but she takes my hand in a show of support.

I take a deep breath, picturing the faces of my family. My mother, father, sister, friends. All dead. But I alone can choose how I honor their memories.

"My little two-leg has taught me about moving on from a difficult past," I say after a long moment. "By clinging to the actions of your ancestors, I risked losing the female who holds my heart. I will accept your apology."

Charlie beams at me as if I alone am responsible for all the stars in the sky.

***

Charlie

I blink open my eyes as something shifts beneath my chest.

"Dragix?"

He smiles down at me, looking perfectly content and one-hundred-percent alive. "Who were you expecting, my little two-leg?"

I laugh at the absurd nickname, and then I lean up and kiss him.

"I missed you so much," I murmur, and it's only when Dragix brushes the tears off my face that I realize I'm crying.

"I missed you too. You left a hole in my heart, Charlie."

"Did you mean what you said?"

He raises an eyebrow, and I blush, suddenly feeling ridiculously awkward.

I glance away, and his hand is gentle as he cups my chin, encouraging me to look at him.

"When you said you loved me," I blurt out. "You were dying, so I won't hold it against you if you didn't mean it."

Dragix suddenly sits up, pulling me up with him. His eyes are blazing gold and very, very serious.

"I meant it more than anything I have said in my life. You are mine, Charlie," he says. He gives me an indulgent smile when I stiffen. "It's okay," he says gently. "I'm yours too. I began mating with you when we were still in my lair. My dragon didn't care about all the reasons we should not be together. It just knew that you were the one I should be with—whether that was for eternity or just a few days."

I stare at him, stunned. "What does it mean if you're my mate?"

"It means that our lives are tied together. Where one goes, the other follows. It means that you are the other half of my soul, and we will never be parted." He hesitates for a moment, looking slightly unsure. "Is this acceptable to you?"

"Acceptable? I love you, Dragix. I knew I loved you that day when you were so injured and we slept under the stars. But I was scared to admit it...even to myself. I'm honored to be your mate, but...what does it mean if our lives are tied together? I know you're not immortal any longer."

Dragix leans down and nuzzles into my neck. My eyes slide closed, and then I force them back open, burying my hands in his hair and pulling his head away.

"You're trying to distract me," I say, and he sighs.

"I fear you will be unhappy with me."

"Uh-oh. Better come clean, buddy."

"When you take your final sleep, I will take mine with you. We will go into the great beyond together."

I stare at him. "Dragix, I might only have fifty or sixty years left. Humans don't age well."

He smiles at me. "I believe you will benefit from some of the immortality I lost. If not, then we will make the most of the time we have."

He shrugs as if he couldn't care less, and I stare at him.

"You're crazy."

"I'm in love." He sighs as if exasperated, and I narrow my eyes at him. "I don't want to live without you. I tried it, and it felt worse than anything I had felt before. I will age with you, and we will take each day as it comes."

"God, Dragix..."

He gives me a slow smile. "I finally have something to live for. Don't mourn for centuries of life as an enraged beast."

I feel like I should protest this decision of his some more, but he moves back, and within moments, he's pulling off the shirt I slept in last night. He lets out a low, very male growl as my breasts pop free.

"I missed these too," he says, leaning down to nuzzle at them. I wind my hands through his hair and sigh against him. His hands slide over my waist, upward, until he's cupping my breasts, his fingers brushing my nipples.

In the blink of an eye, his hands fall away, and he locks his arms beneath my butt, hauling me into them. He lifts me, obviously planning to head toward the bed. But he pauses as my breasts hang in his face, and then he's kissing them, his tongue flicking over my nipple as I let out a low, rough groan.

He moves to my other breast, using slightly more teeth this time, and I shudder in his arms.

"You're driving me crazy."

"As I should."

I blink at that, and then I'm flat on my back, gazing up at him. He kneels over me, pulling off my pants. Then he pauses, his gaze like a brand as he takes in my body. His eyes meet mine, and the breath leaves my lungs at the pure *need* in those golden orbs.

He lowers his head to mine and kisses me, so gentle, so careful, even as he shudders above me. I can feel his desperation, but he takes his time, caressing my lips.

He rests more of his weight on me, his cock lining up with where I need him the most. He grinds slightly against me as if he can't help himself, and I tilt my hips.

"You're so wet," he gasps, moving his lips to my neck.

"So don't leave me waiting."

He laughs, his breath warm against my throat. "Never."

He presses inside me, and I groan at the feel of every inch of him. Once he's all the way inside me, he pauses, dropping gentle kisses over every inch of my face.

He thrusts gently, getting me used to the size of him again. But I'm more than ready for him, and I wrap my legs around his waist, angling so he can move deeper, harder.

He complies, thrusting faster, undulating into me so he can hit the spot that makes me tighten around him. The one that makes my head fall back. He growls at that and hits it again, and warm golden pleasure unfurls throughout my body as I gasp, trembling through my climax.

He draws out my orgasm, continuing his steady pumping. "We're not done," he tells me, and then he puts his hands under my butt and deftly flips us until I'm sitting on top.

I blink at him, still half lost in the afterglow of my orgasm, but he reaches for my nipple, tweaking it, and then slides his hand possessively down my body until he finds my clit.

I'm so sensitive that I gasp, clenching around him, and he groans.

He lifts his hips, and I move, placing my hands on his chest for leverage. My nails dig into his skin, but from the way he gasps, I can tell he likes it. He uses his fingertip to run light circles around my clit, and my moans turn to one long wail as he rubs faster and I slam down on him, shuddering as I come so hard I see black spots.

Distantly, I can hear him growl out his own climax as he shifts both hands to my butt, thrusting a few more times. I collapse on top of him, and we both attempt to catch our breath.

"You know, this is crazy," I murmur. "I was abducted, crash-landed on an alien planet, and fell in love with a dragon."

His eyes gleam gold, heavy with satisfaction as he pulls me closer.

"Of course you did," he says, arrogance coating every word.

Charlie

I soar through the sky on my dragon's back, laughing as he arrows down toward the Colossal Water.

I squeal as he lowers his claws and water sprays up at me, but it feels cool and refreshing on my skin.

He rises, and I lean forward. "Again!"

Dragix's laugh echoes in my head, and this time he goes deeper, flicking his tail until I'm drenched.

I gasp, and he lets out a rumble—the equivalent to a dragon howling with laughter.

"You think you're real funny, don't you?"

He snorts, and I grin.

I'm ridiculously happy.

We head toward Dragix's territory, and I close my eyes as he angles down to where a herd of animals is grazing.

I grimace at the sickening crunch as he eats one of them, but I know he has several more held carefully in his claws.

We head back toward Rakiz's camp, and people glance up as Dragix flies low, his winged form casting a huge shadow over the camp. He reaches the small, empty clearing near the cooking kradi and drops his offering on the ground.

One of the cooks gives him a pleased wave.

Now that there are so many extra human women staying here, there are even more mouths to feed. Dragix has taken it upon himself to help contribute the extra meat, which frees up some of Rakiz's hunters to instead look for any remaining Dokhalls.

Maez is waiting for us when we land near the camp entrance. She has become fast friends with Ellie. And while she sometimes comes back to Dragix's lair with us when we want some time alone, she's spending more and more time hanging out at camp.

Dragix gives me a slow smile as he transforms, and my stomach muscles clench in anticipation.

"I need to go talk to Zoey," I tell him. *"I'll meet you in our kradi later?"*

He nods, turning to talk to Maez. *"Don't be too long, little two-leg. I crave you."*

I send him a smile over my shoulder and add a swish of my hips as I stroll away, laughing at the deep groan he sends down our mental pathway.

I find Zoey in the healers' kradi. We've gotten close over the past few weeks, and I often hang out with her, Vivian, and Vivian's cousin Sarissa. They haven't yet gone to Arix for help fixing their ship. Some of the human women were injured, and Sarissa wants to wait until they're all healed properly before she leaves.

I think she's been nominated as their unofficial leader, and she seems to take the job seriously, constantly checking in with each of the women throughout the day.

"Oh, hey." Zoey smiles at me. She's currently working next to Moni, one of the healers. Since Zoey was a nurse on Earth, she's fascinated with the different healing methods on Agron, and she's been learning everything she can. Something is going on with her though. Recently, she's been withdrawn, secretive, and...sad.

She leans over and murmurs to Moni and then follows me out of the kradi. She knows I prefer to be away from the healers, from the heady scent of herbs that remind me of being slumped over Dragix's unconscious body while I waited to see if he would live or die.

The sun is warm on my skin, and I enjoy the fresh breeze as we walk toward the large clearing where most of the Braxian kids hang out.

"How are you doing?" I ask.

Zoey shrugs. "I'm okay." I raise my eyebrow, and she laughs. "I am, really. I'm just...at a loss, I guess. I'm so used to being helpful and *needed* on Earth. Here, I feel like nothing but a burden."

My mouth drops open at that. "Are you kidding me?" I had no idea she was feeling this way. "You're not a burden at all, Zoey." She sighs, and I give her a look. "You're not."

"It's just...you guys are all out there, kicking ass and taking names. Nevada's got her sword, Beth has her crossbow, Ivy has her knife, you have your bloodthirsty dragon..."

I burst out laughing, and she frowns at me but rolls her eyes with a chuckle.

"I know, I hear myself."

I stop her with a hand on her arm and examine her face. She's looking better than she has since I've known her, her face flushed with health, her breathing steady. "Where is this coming from?"

"I was a trauma nurse at home. I was so used to being in

control all the time. I was used to being someone who had her shit together. Who could be counted on. Here, I've just been nothing but a captive and then a patient."

Telling her that no one sees her that way won't help at all, if that's how she truly feels.

"Okay," I say. "What are you going to do about it?"

She gives me such a grateful look that it's clear that this is the right question to ask.

"I want to learn to fight. Tagiz won't teach me—big surprise—so I've asked Hewex. He's not exactly keen on the idea, but I'm working on him." Her pretty face shines with determination.

I nod. "That sounds like a great idea."

She raises her eyebrow. "Really? You're not just saying that?"

"If that's what you feel like you need to do to feel safer, to feel like you're more in control, then I say go for it. I have one question for you though."

"Yes?"

"Are you sure you're doing this for yourself and not to prove to a certain overprotective warrior that you're not fragile?"

She laughs, and heads turn, more than one set of Braxian lips tilting up at the joyous sound.

"Okay," she admits. "That's definitely part of it. But it's not the only reason, I promise."

I link arms with her, and we begin walking back toward the kradis.

"In that case, I think you should go for it. Life is short. Plus, if that ship gets fixed, you'll have to decide if you're staying here or not. Why not make the most of the time you have here?"

Zoey smiles. "You're so wise."

I grin. "It's easier to give advice than it is to receive it."

I leave her back at the healers' kradi and make my way to my own, my thighs clenching in anticipation.

Dragix is already waiting for me.

Naked.

I let out a yelp of surprise as he pounces, scooping me into his arms in a move so fast that he's almost a blur. Then I'm blinking up at him as he grins down at me.

"You took too long," he growls, but his lips are twitching.

"You're not the center of the universe, you know."

"Is that right?"

He tickles me, and I howl with laughter, attempting to fight him off.

Then he pulls at the laces of my dress, and his amusement turns to pure lust.

"You're so beautiful," he murmurs.

I smile, dragging him closer, and my eyes flutter shut as he kisses his way down my neck.

He saw me. And he took me.

And I couldn't be happier.

The End

Author's note:

There are some novels that come together perfectly, based on a plan or an outline I created in my head months earlier. There are others that require head-scratching and long days spent staring at my computer as I get past a particularly difficult scene or chapter.

Charlie and Dragix's story doesn't fit into either of these categories.

Occasionally, I have two characters who insist on telling *their* stories, 100% of the time. And I'm just along for the ride. Charlie's abusive ex? That was news to me. But she insisted I tell her whole story, to highlight all of the reasons why she is the women she is today.

And Dragix? He is one bossy dragon.

I hope you enjoyed Captured by the Alien Warrior as much as I enjoyed writing it. Next up is Zoey and Tagiz's story in Rescued by the Alien Warrior.

Want to be the first to know about freebies, new releases and sales? Sign up for my free newsletter at www.hopehartauthor.com

And don't forget to come say hi on Facebook- Hope Hart Author.

ALSO BY HOPE HART

The Arcav Alien Invasion Series

The Arcav King's Mate

The Arcav Commander's Human

The Arcav General's Woman

The Arcav Prince's Captive

A Very Arcav Christmas

The Arcav Captain's Queen

The Arcav Guard's Female

The Warriors of Agron Series

Taken by the Alien Warrior

Claimed by the Alien Warrior

Saved by the Alien Warrior

Seduced by the Alien Warrior

Protected by the Alien Warrior

Captured by the Alien Warrior

Rescued by the Alien Warrior

Enticed by the Alien Warrior